The Endless Dark

STORIES OF UNDERGROUND ADVENTURE

Other Collections by Phyllis R. Fenner

Behind the Wheel
Stories of Cars on Road and Track

Consider the Evidence
Stories of Mystery and Suspense

Contraband
Stories of Smuggling the World Over

Desperate Moments
Stories of Escapes and Hurried Journeys

Finders Keepers
Stories of Treasure Seekers

Full Forty Fathoms
Stories of Underwater Adventure

Gentle Like a Cyclone
Stories of Horses and Their Riders

Lift Line
Stories of Downhill and Cross-Country Skiing

No Time for Glory
Stories of World War II

Open Throttle
Stories of Railroads and Railroad Men

Perilous Ascent
Stories of Mountain Climbing

Where Speed Is King
Stories of Racing Adventure

THE ENDLESS DARK

Stories of Underground Adventure

SELECTED BY

Phyllis R. Fenner

ILLUSTRATED BY STEVE MARCHESI

WILLIAM MORROW AND COMPANY
NEW YORK / 1977

Copyright © 1977 by Phyllis R. Fenner

Grateful acknowledgment is made for permission to reprint the following:
"Treasure Trap" by Don Waters. Copyright 1945 by The Curtis Publishing
Company. Originally published in *The Saturday Evening Post.*
"Dark Flowers" by Kay Haugaard from *Teen-Age Ghost Stories,* copyright
1961. Reprinted by permission of Lantern Press, Inc.
"The Problem Solver and the Spy" by Christopher Anvil. Copyright © 1965
by Davis Publications, Inc. Originally published in *Ellery Queen's Mystery
Magazine.* Reprinted by permission of the author and his agents, Scott Mere-
dith Literary Agency, Inc., 845 Third Avenue, New York 10022.
"Lost in the Caverns" by William L. Gresham. Copyright 1951 by The Curtis
Publishing Company, Inc. Originally published in *The Saturday Evening
Post.* Reprinted by permission of Brandt & Brandt.
"Underground Episode" by Edmund Ware Smith. Copyright 1934 by Story
Magazine, Inc. Originally published in *Story Magazine.* Reprinted by per-
mission of Brandt & Brandt.
"The Cave" by P. Schuyler Miller. Copyright 1942 by Street & Smith Publi-
cations, Inc., copyright renewed 1970 by The Condé Nast Publications, Inc.
Reprinted by permission of the author and The Condé Nast Publications, Inc.
"Lindbergh and the Underground Lake" by Robert F. Burgess from *The
Cave Divers,* copyright © 1976 by Robert F. Burgess. Reprinted by permis-
sion of Dodd, Mead & Company, Inc.
"The Bottomless Well" by Walter S. Terry. Copyright © 1965 by the Uni-
versity of Georgia. Originally published in *The Georgia Review.* Reprinted by
permission of the author and *The Georgia Review.*
"The Virgin Cave" by Bryce Walton. Copyright © 1965 by Davis Publications, Inc. Originally published in *Ellery Queen's Mystery Magazine.* Reprinted by permission of the author and his agent, Raines & Raines.
"The Lost Continent" by Geoffrey Household. Copyright 1960 by Geoffrey
Household. Originally published in *The Saturday Evening Post.* Reprinted by
permission of Brandt & Brandt.

Printed in the United States of America.
Design by Victoria Gomez.

1   2   3   4   5   6   7   8   9   10

Library of Congress Cataloging in Publication Data

Main entry under title:

The Endless dark.

SUMMARY: Ten short stories about cave exploration
and other underground adventures.
1. Caves—Juvenile fiction. 2. Short stories. [1. Caves—Fiction.
2. Short stories]   I. Fenner, Phyllis Reid, (date)   II. Marchesi, Steve.
PZ5.E54   [Fic]   77-5494
ISBN 0-688-22122-X   ISBN 0-688-32122-4 lib. bdg.

Contents

For
NANCY AND MARTIN,
who came out of my need.

A Dark World

Imagine a world without light, with unchanging temperature, motionless air and water, and total silence. That is the cave world. Sometimes there are long, narrow tunnels, enormous rooms, and even lakes in this mysterious world. There may be living things, such as bats and sightless fish and insects. Occasionally things of great beauty and remnants of earlier times are found. The Dead Sea Scrolls were found in a cave as well as hardened-mud objects and wall paintings made by primitive man. The very word *cave* makes one think of mystery, adventure, beauty, and danger.

Why do people feel the lure of caves? Cavers,

9

spelunkers, speleologists—whatever they are called —are impelled by the excitement of discovery and exploration, the sight of something that no one else has ever seen before.

Cavers must have curiosity, endurance, courage, patience, team spirit (for one should never explore caves alone), a sense of direction, and a level head. They are exploring a new, secret world.

P.F.

Treasure Trap

DON WATERS

John Pindar stood beside the wheel, idly holding his schooner on her course as she leisurely ran off before a light northeaster. He pulled the palm-plait hat he wore down over his forehead and through half-closed eyes looked ahead at the sun glint dancing on the water.

Timmy Albury, sitting on the rail beside him, spoke dolefully. "So we lost not only the money for the hauling, but we're out a lot more for the damages on our last trip."

A worried note was in his voice when John Pindar answered. "That bit of a blow that we met up with in the Northeast Providence Channel hit me harder

11

than it did the *Tiburon*. When the main-hatch tarpaulin split and let the water leak onto our cargo, the flour and sugar got soaked. Malone claims they were almost all spoiled. He says the canned goods with the water-stained labels are hard to sell. The tins are rust spotted, the—"

Timmy interrupted him. "But he didn't say the flour will be as good as ever, except for a thin crust next to the sacks. The water wouldn't soak in for more than a quarter of an inch. The tinned goods—" He paused, shook his head. "Why, half the stuff on his shelves is rust streaked. I've never known him to knock a penny off the selling price on that account."

John Pindar glanced up at the peak of the main gaff and down at the water alongside before answering. "That's business, Timmy, and he's a good businessman. In all my dealings with him, I've seldom got the best of the bargain. In fact, most of the time I've been lucky to break even, and many of the deals have gone in his favor. Yet I'll say this for him: once he makes a bargain, he sticks by it. But he's generally pretty certain he stands to profit before he gives his word."

He gazed ahead, off to the eastward, at the white limestone cliffs of an island with a fringe of bushy-topped coconut palms that ran along its crest like a mane, at the flock of man-of-war birds sailing above, from which the cay got its name.

He turned back to his companion and resumed his conversation. "Malone made me a proposition. He offered to sell the load to me for twenty-five percent less than what *he* paid for it and take the loss himself. Or I could stand the twenty-five percent damage. That took the haul bill and more besides. Sell or buy; on the face of it, that looked as though it was a fair deal."

John Pindar laughed scornfully. "Oh, he was safe in that! He well knew I didn't have the money to take him up. Had he realized the new suit of sails the schooner now wears has not yet been paid for or that the last bill at the shipyard is long since overdue, he might have turned the screws down tighter. It's a hard game, this trying to make an honest living with a small sailing vessel. And now we're on another trip for him. If this one doesn't pay off—"

"But," Timmy hopefully reminded him, "there's always the chance a bit of luck will come our way. Remember the time when we ran across those drums of gasoline some steamer lost from her deckload during heavy weather?" He chuckled. "The sea's surface was peppered with them. Two hundred, wasn't it, we saved?" he asked.

John Pindar nodded. "Two hundred. We cleared a couple of thousand dollars then. But that has been several years gone now. Since then we've netted sharks in the passes and fished on the reef, gathered conch shells and sponges, hauled coconuts from Andros and salt from Inagua, a load of cattle from Turk's Island and provisions for Conch Cay. A lot of work and little gain."

13

He moved the wheel down a couple of spokes, and the schooner swung to avoid a brown spot in the clear water that denoted a clump of weed-grown rocks below. He settled her back on her course, the bowsprit heading straight for the island, before he continued again. "Yes, we've sweated in flat calms in midsummer, been dismasted by a hurricane in the fall, fought a nor'easter across the Gulf Stream, and beat back and forth for slow, hot days over the banks in light weather. And for what?" he exclaimed bitterly, and gave his own answer. "For a meager wage."

Timmy answered, "Oh, we'll make it all right, John. Something is bound to turn up. It's always darkest just before dawn."

A quietness fell on the two men as the *Tiburon* slowly forged along the pea-green water toward where the rocky shores of the approaching island were outlined against the velvet blue of a cloudless sky. The low gurgle of water swirling around the rudder post and sliding along the bilge, the small creak of a line in a block, the half-heard rustling of the wind alone broke the stillness punctuated by the faint boom of the surf on the reef a mile away.

After a long silence, John Pindar's voice arose. "We're not beaten till we're down and out. Let's see how that goes. A man is never down and out. When he wears the soles from his shoes, he's on his feet again."

Both laughed and glanced down at their bare feet.

14

But there was little merriment in their glum faces. The cay gradually drew nearer. The wind was lightening. The schooner barely had steerage on now.

John Pindar remarked, "Well, the breeze has about petered out. We'll come to anchor. It probably will be after sundown before we get wind enough to work out through the pass." He pointed toward the beach, now hardly a quarter of a mile off. "We'll go ashore and pick up a few crawfish for dinner."

When the *Tiburon* was within a few hundred yards of the island, he rolled the wheel. Her head swung and she faced the wind. Timmy's feet pattered along the deck in a broken rhythm as he went forward, limping slightly from an old injury. The anchor fell from the cathead with a splash. Jib and staysail, fore and main fluttered down stay and mast. A few minutes later they got into the dinghy trailing astern and sculled it ashore.

With his two-tined spear in his hand, John Pindar eased through the water along the rock shore. Every now and then he jabbed the gig down, the long pole vibrated, and, flipping violently, a big spiny lobster was lifted out from a hole in the rocks below. He turned to where Timmy held an open sack in his hands.

"There's enough now," he said. "You'd better go out to the *Tiburon* and get them boiled for dinner. I'll give you a call when I want to leave here. I think I'll look around on the cliff and see if any of the egg birds have laid yet."

15

He made his way back along the thin strip of beach that separated the rocky wall of Man-of-War Cay from the low-water mark. He stopped, watched the bent figure, the sack over his back, walking in a long-and-short step. Timmy shoved the dinghy afloat, settled the oar in the notch in its transom, and, with an easy lunge and swing, sculled it out toward where the *Tiburon* lay.

They'd been through a lot together, and Timmy had stuck by him faithfully through fair weather and foul. He felt a sense of incompetency when he thought of how little the other had made since the day the schooner had been launched. He was getting old; the injury he'd got during a hurricane on board bothered him at times now. If the *Tiburon* could just make a few paying voyages, Timmy could fix up the little place he owned and get his home in shape for the day that was not far off when he'd no longer be able to go to sea.

The wind had died and a flat calm lay on the water. The schooner's anchor chain hung limp and pendent from her hawspipe. The water on which she floated was so transparent that it seemed as though she were suspended in the air. The sky behind her was a light robin's-egg blue on which her outline was etched clear and sharp in the brilliant sunshine. For a brief second a misgiving ran through John Pindar. Had he wasted his time? Would he have been better off in some other business? Malone, with his store on Conch Cay, was well off. He'd made it all buying and selling, bartering and trading. He slept in a comfortable bed at night and never had to take the risks of the sea. And when age overtook him, he'd not have to worry about poverty.

John Pindar turned and climbed up the sloping face of the cliff till he stood thirty feet above the water. He drew a deep breath. The scene before him was one to make any man pause and look. The soft pastel shades of brown and orange shaded into velvety green and merged into azure as the waters deepened. Out to the eastward, the slow deep-sea surges rose, seemed to pause, then with a slow boom broke into creaming lather on the coral reef. Beyond the breakers, the ocean stretched out till it met, in the far distance, a faint line where sky and water appeared welded to each other.

As he stood there, he realized he never could be happy cooped up by four walls, peddling things across the counter. This was his life, out where the wind rattled the dried fronds of the coco palms, out where the waves broke on the coral heads, where he could feel the hand-polished grip of a wheel or the rough rasp of a mainsheet in his hands.

He took a few steps, bent over, and picked up a conch shell lying in a cleft in the rocks. Its end was smooth, its lip chipped and broken. He recognized it as one of the tools left behind by men who no longer lived here. He'd often found shells like this on the beaches along these islands. The Lucayans, the original inhabitants, had used them for hand tools. With the conch for a scraper and fire for a helper, they built their dugout canoes in which they traveled from place to place across these purple waters.

He wondered if life had been easy for them. Food was plentiful; their crude tools and meager equipment were all they needed to cope with a mild climate. Then there came the time when the high-pooped galleons of Spain had anchored off these isolated cays. The tough and merciless fighting men of Castile had come ashore avid for treasure, and the Lucayans had been exterminated.

John Pindar dropped the shell and walked along the ledge. A cloud of seabirds mewed and cried above him. He scanned the little shelflike projections along the rocks. The birds had gathered, but as yet had not begun to lay. From boulder to boulder, he made his way down again toward the beach.

As he reached it, he noticed a hole in the face of the cliff, a strong stream of water running out from it. He'd never seen this cave before, although he had been on Man-of-War often, gigging crawfish. Then the reason he had not come on this until now became apparent. Last night was full moon and the tide was very low. At normal water level this opening was submerged.

He glanced inside. The cavern extended back into the darkness so far that he could not see its end. Suddenly an idea was born in his mind. He'd heard the old tales of wealth concealed on this cay, tales that no doubt had grown in the telling. For this string of islands along the Abaco coast had known many men: rumrunner and buccaneer, pirate and freebooter. British and French and Spaniard had one after the other fought and robbed, murdered and pillaged, drunk and caroused, and even at times, when hard pressed, had hidden their loot.

John Pindar felt in his pockets. He pulled out the bottle in which he kept his matches dry. A couple of windblown palm fronds lay in a crack in the rocks. He twisted a bundle of the leaves together and struck a match to them. In the wavering light from his torch, he ducked his head and looked inside. The cave opened up into a spacious room with a pool for a floor. Overhead was a rocky roof, well studded with stalactites from which the water dripped.

He stepped in and walked along the narrow corridor. The water deepened; it covered his hips, then came up to his armpits. Holding his torch high, he followed the passageway. It bent around a turn; the bright glare from the opening behind him disappeared. The enclosed gorge pinched in on either side. The roof sloped down till, just at the edge of his illumination, the slab of rock angled down to the water.

He started to turn back, but hesitated. His torch had burned down to a stub. It appeared as though this cleft stopped. Then he felt a gentle current against his body. The water was running through from farther back. This passage was not closed.

The burning palm leaves guttered out. He tossed

19

the glowing end away, caught his breath, and dived under. His hands scraped the wall on either side. He reached up after half a dozen strokes and could not feel the ceiling above him.

His head emerged. He lowered his feet, but the water was too deep for him to reach bottom. He swam for another dozen strokes and then tried again. It was shallow here, and he waded ahead till he was out of the water and his bare feet trod on a pebble beach. He shook himself and took the knife he carried from its sheath in his belt. Holding it by its blade, he swished it back and forth to dry it. With his teeth, he pulled the cork out of the bottle and shook out a match. Then he struck it on the rough, shark-skin-covered handle of his knife. In its feeble glare, he looked straight ahead . . . into a grinning skull not a foot in front of his face.

John Pindar started. Wedged into a cleft was the skeleton of a man, gray-green with age. Quickly he surveyed it—a squat man who must have been broad across the shoulders, heavily muscled; without a doubt, one of the aboriginals who had lived on these scattered islands when the first white men arrived. Just a hand's reach away, lying face down, was another skeleton, a rusty sword between its ribs.

Before the match burned down, he knew this was no savage. The remains of a buckle, even the few moldly shreds of cloth that draped the bones, showed that more than likely some soldier of Spain had breathed his last here. They had left many relics of their stay on these cays—bits of rusty iron, cannon-balls, hilts of broken swords—reminders that once this country of rocky islands and pea-green water had been a part of the far-flung Spanish colonial empire. These two had been dead and hidden in this tomb for at least a couple of centuries.

By the light of another match, he saw lying in front of those age-stained bones a big conch shell. The knob on its end had been cut off, the hole stopped with a plug—a hard, dense tropical wood that had withstood the slow disintegration of time. As he reached out and picked it up, a faint rattle issued from it. His match died and the darkness enveloped him. He twisted the plug out and turned the shell up. Into his cupped hand below he felt a stream of round, hard pellets fall. Without the aid of his eyes he knew these were no pebbles. They were smooth and velvety, sleek to his touch. With difficulty he lit another match, and its light showed them gleaming dully, a handful of pearls that glistened green and purple, bronze and amber.

He rolled them around in his palm. Evidently they had not been damaged by the passing of time, enclosed as they were in their crude case. His heart beat fast. He held a treasure in his hand. A smile of complete satisfaction swept over his face.

His thoughts turned to the storekeeper. Malone had put it over on him for the last time. These pearls would readily sell in Miami and no doubt bring a fine price. He'd have the money then he now lacked. Ah, that was it. How easy it would be to go into the store at Conch Cay, pull a long face, talk about heavy weather and the difficulties of keeping the cargo dry. Malone would immediately jump to the conclusion that the same thing had happened again, and he'd make the same proposition. Buy or sell; he'd either take the cargo as is, at his own figure, or dispose of it at the same price. He wouldn't even bother to examine it. He would be sure that John Pindar could not buy, and he would set the sum low.

John Pindar turned. There was nothing more to keep him here. He dropped the pearls into his dungarees' pocket and buttoned it, waded into the water, dived, headed to where he was certain the passage lay. His groping fingers met only the smooth, wet rocks. He caught his breath and tried it again, with the same result. He'd lost his sense of direction. There was nothing here by which a man could tell east or west, north or south. He dived again and again, but without coming upon that narrow cleft. The cold, clammy air of the cavern seemed to be enveloping him in a shroud. There was no sound but his own breathing. Each heartbeat thumped loud in his ears. He must get out. Time after time he plunged down, only to come up against the hard stone.

Frantically he clawed his way around the edge of the pool, feeling, probing for that hole through which he had entered. The place was a couple of hundred feet across, and the chances of blindly discovering the small break were slim. He was used to working underwater on the reef, but out there man rose to the fresh air and bright sunshine, caught his breath clean and sweet in the warm drift of the trade wind. Here the air above was as black as the water below, a fetid atmosphere that held the chill of death.

He waded out into the pool and struck a match. It sputtered, almost died out, then flared up. He'd have to be careful now. His matches were beginning to get damp from handling, and there were but two left. He held his hand up and gazed intently at the surface below him. It was dead flat, except where a little ripple swept across it when he moved. Two matches, two little slivers of wood tipped with phosphorus, and when they were gone, he'd have nothing to break the darkness around him.

A blind and unreasoning panic overtook him. To be sealed up here in the everlasting night, to be cut off from the sunshine was terrifying. The blackness pressed closer and closer on him. The silence was absolute. Not the faintest whisper of sound from the outside penetrated here. He was cut off from the world of men. These dripping rocks were a dungeon, a cell with a door sealed tight, hidden underwater.

Scarcely stopping between dives, he plunged down and came up. His fingers scraped against the soft slime, his hands blindly pressed against the limestone. The pool sloped down steeply from the beach to a seemingly bottomless hole. Time had ceased to exist. There was no way now to mark the passing of the hours. He swam underwater, round and round, driven by a desperate urge. The opening he came through had vanished completely. Not even a small fissure, not the slightest place where a break occurred met his search.

His shoulder muscles were tired, his breath came in gasps. Finally he calmed down and reasoned with himself. He'd never escape unless he kept his head. He felt the pebbles of the beach under his feet and realized with a shock that the tide was rising. He'd come in at low water. The flow had been out then. Now it had reversed. He stood for a long time thinking while the water crept up past his knees. All around him the walls came straight down, except in that one place where the ledge jutted out. He climbed up on it, sat crouched over, his hands clasped around his knees; sat close to where a couple of other men had been up against the same hopeless situation. They had failed.

In his mind he reenacted what probably had happened. That native, hotly pursued by the man with the sword, had found his way in here with his treasure. The other had followed. How long had they lasted with nothing but salt water to drink? The squat, heavy-shouldered fellow crouched back in the niche had died of fear. The dark to him was peopled with malignant spirits that surrounded him and, in his imagination, clutched and menaced with invisible hands.

The man with the sharp steel blade— How long had he waited before he'd fallen on his upright weapon and ended the agony of his body weakened by hunger, his mind crazed by thirst? Those two had come in here, one driven by fear, the other by greed. Neither had gone out. Now he decided he would not linger here day after slow day, beating futilely against those rocks. He had his sheath knife, and he'd use it on himself.

That, though, could wait. It was the final expedient when all else failed. Perhaps he might be able to detect the current coming in as he had felt it going out in the other cavern. Anything was better than sitting waiting. He tried floating on his back, lying still, but he seemed to stay in the same place. That was no help. He hauled himself back onto the ledge again, alone in the darkness with his thoughts, the sound of his own breathing and the dripping of water from his dungarees keeping him company.

The hours passed. He'd been in here since almost noon. He reached over to the water a couple of feet below him. If the tide had not already turned to ebb, it soon would swirl around the end of the island, eddy among the rocks off the point, and then, like a fast-running river, race out through the pass, out through the break in the reef, and lose its force in the dark blue of the sea.

His mind ranged back over the years. He recalled working with his father out on the reef. He'd learned to dive then, stripping the copper and brass from a wrecked steamer that lay in six fathoms just on the outside of the coral wall. The *Tiburon*—his schooner

25

that he'd left anchored out there in the bright sunshine. He remembered the work he'd put in, building her, getting the timbers out from the woods, hewing keel and frame, driving driftbolts, ripping planking, sewing sails, splicing rigging. He'd put a lot of himself into that vessel.

He thought of the cargoes he'd hauled for Malone. A sickening sense of finality came over him. Was that his last trip? All his ideas of revenge were gone. They were so futile now. He was up against something that dwarfed all those plans into insignificance. He slid into the water. As his feet struck the bottom, he knew the tide was more than halfway out. The current should be swift outside and running out of this pool fast.

Gradually it came over him. That stream of water flowing out the entrance could be his guide. He had only to find it. He carefully set his small match bottle down, propped against the moldering bones on the shelf. He took the cork out, methodically shaved it into small pieces with his knife, catching them into his hands. He waded out till the water was shoulder high. Then he let the little crumbs of cork fall from his outstretched fingers. Slowly he backed away, moving gently, inch by inch, so as not to create any disturbance.

He reached the edge of the gravel beach, leaned against the wall, and waited. The long minutes passed. Several times he started away, but forced himself to remain where he was. It seemed like eternity as the tide crept down on his legs, till the water he stood in was but ankle deep.

Finally he moved and felt cautiously behind him among the bones till his fingers touched the bottle. With his knife blade in his teeth and the glass held high, he eased out into the pond. It was hard to resist the temptation to hurry his progress.

At last he was almost shoulder deep. In spite of his efforts to control himself, his hands were shaking as he took a match from its container. He rasped it across the knife handle a half dozen times before it sputtered. Holding his breath, he watched the feeble flame in its tip glow, brighten, and then die. He had one match left, one more chance. He hesitated before he struck it with trembling fingers. The wood caught and a little blob of light wavered, flickered, and burst into flame.

He gazed down. The cork he had dropped was not in sight. Perhaps he had waited too long. Perhaps it had drifted with the flow and been sucked under and out of sight. He turned around, the tiny torch high over his head. Then he saw the bits of cork floating on the black water. They had scattered and spread into a crescent-shaped line. He barely caught a glimpse of that break in the smooth ebony beneath when his match went out.

The darkness closed down again. Yet in that brief instant before the light had been extinguished, he

27

had got the hint that he needed. Straight in front of him, the bulge of the curve showed the direction of the current. He began swimming, dived.

His hands were outstretched before him when one shoulder struck the rocks. He'd found the opening. A few swift drives of arms and legs, and he raised himself up.

Ahead, a dim glow blossomed like a flower painted on a velvet background. He turned the corner in the passage. The mouth of the cave came in sight, and framed in its jagged circle the outlines of the schooner were etched like a silhouette in the path of the moonlight. He stepped out on the beach and drew in a long breath of clean, fresh air.

Above the booming of the offshore reef, he heard Timmy hoarsely calling in a tone of despair, "John! Oh, John!"

He threw back his head, and loud and clear his own voice rose in answer.

Dark Flowers

KAY HAUGAARD

The rubes were being herded into the dark opening one by one. Clad in their shapeless overalls and huge black galoshes, they resembled a herd of silent gray elephants.

Greta Lindgren waited impatiently for her friend Dick Thomas to guide the last ponderously garbed tourist through the uninviting opening before she started down the steep metal steps into the cave. Entering from the golden sunshine of the summer day, it seemed darker, even damper, with a chill that clung like a clammy blanket.

"Watch your step, ladies and gentlemen. I will not

29

deceive you into thinking the caves are entirely safe. The ladders are slippery and so are the paths."

Dick reached up and took the hand of a woman whose gray hair was frizzed into little knots. She was clutching her enormous flower-covered straw purse incongruously against her tarpaulinlike overalls. She appeared frightened.

"As long as you do not stray from the regular path and watch your step carefully, there is nothing to fear, ma'am." Dick brought the woman safely down from the ladder onto the damp dirt path beside him.

Greta ducked her head automatically to avoid a low-hanging stalactite. She had followed Dick through on these tours so many times during her time off from her job at the gift shop that she practically knew his spiel by heart. Her first trip through at the beginning of June, when she had just arrived to work for the summer, had awed and terrified her. Now she felt she could grope her way under the stalactites and between the stalagmites (stalactites stick "tite" to the ceiling, stalagmites "mite" if they could, she remembered, feeling immensely clever that she had), between the pillars, down the ladders, up the ladders, over the Frozen Lake, through the Great Hall, down the Catacomb Corridor, and out into the daylight without even the assistance of a flashlight.

The group of tourists walked down the narrow dirt path that edged a deep chasm filled with an angry, jagged mass of rock made menacingly alive by the shifting finger of shadow caused by Dick's swinging lantern.

"On your left, ladies and gentlemen, you will see Dante's Inferno. It has been so named because of its imagined similarity to the Pit. If you look closely, you will see the glow of the fires." Dick flicked a switch with his boot, and the whole bottom of the cavern lit up with a red glow of varied intensity, from a hot, searing red in the open light to warm blacks deepened, reddened to blood color in the shadows.

There were *ooh*'s and *aah*'s from the tourists. Dick continued with his speech, catching sight of Greta and winking at her openly now that all other heads were directed toward the chasm. "Of course, ladies and gentlemen, this bit of fantasy is a miracle of modern science and one with which we are all familiar. But there is a story about the caves that does not have such a simple explanation. It concerns a young girl named Augusta Guthrie, who was passing through this country with her family during the early 1870's in a wagon train."

Then Dick retold the tale Greta knew so well. She had heard it so often that as she leaned against the jagged wall, her arms crossed tightly against the cold, she was not sure whether she was really hearing Dick's voice or hearing her memory of it.

"She wandered off into the woods by herself. The members of the wagon train were able to follow her footsteps to the mouth of the caves, and they searched throughout the portions of the cave they could reach but with no success. She was never found. She is known as the discoverer of the caves. Some say that she is a jealous owner who has not entirely relinquished her treasure even in death. Many persons whose integrity is respected have sworn they have seen her walking through the higher chambers of the caves, her long calico skirt and sunbonnet ribbons floating in the windless, lightless cave. To some she merely beckons. Others she approaches and asks plaintively, 'Will they yet return?' and lays a bony hand on them in pleading."

Greta smiled a little and looked down at her oxfords, crossed as she leaned against the cave wall. She felt slightly superior to these openmouthed creatures, staring so eagerly and swallowing so gullibly. Perhaps they would laugh when they returned to the coffee shop, but now the air seemed heavier, thicker, wet with silent apprehension.

Then a man broke in with a nervous laugh. "Pretty good story, son." He turned to the others. "They just have to throw in a little show for the money, don't they?"

The others laughed with relief.

Greta looked up to Dick for what she knew he would say. He was a wonderful showman. He rose a little above them on the trail ahead and spoke. His voice gathered small enlarging echoes from the huge cave. "The gentleman is right," he said solemnly.

32

"It's wrong to think of this story too seriously. I try not to think of it as I walk the caves alone. Let's go on to other, more pleasant aspects."

Greta thought maybe she wouldn't walk the whole fifty steps up the steel ladder to the Cathedral, as one small side chamber off the Great Hall was called because of the massive formations that had grown together into groups of towering, translucent pillars resembling a massive pipe organ. She stood at the bottom of the steps as the others walked up slowly. Then, when she was the only one below, Dick called down the ladder, "Young lady, please do not become separated from the group. I could not be responsible for your safety then."

Greta smiled at him and his little game, and at the amused titter that spread among the tourists. He wasn't fooling anyone. So she went up and stood packed into the tiny room with the others, and she listened to his speech while the green lights placed behind the translucent pillars lit the whole thing up like a huge jukebox. The green color gave it an eerie quality. Then, as Dick flicked the switch, a flood of music came from the concealed record player, "I Know a Green Cathedral." This song had always bothered Greta, so she decided to kibitz a bit. "But guide, the green cathedral in the song is a forest."

Dick loosed one of his imperturable grins. "Speak to the management, young lady. I only work here."

Another amused and knowing titter.

At last they had gone through the Great Hall, and

33

Dick turned out all the lights to show what absolute, total, and complete darkness really is or how Jonah must have felt under similar circumstances. There was the ritual of lighting the single match and seeing the huge vault of the cavern come alive with warmth and light and the enormously elongated, writhing shadows of people. Then over the Frozen Lake, down the Catacomb Corridor, and home again, home again, jiggety jig.

Greta was glad because she was tired of stamping her feet and blowing on her hands to keep warm.

Dick came up to her and took her by the arm. "Hey, rube, let's go get rid of this lamp of mine, and we'll see what's for lunch down in ye olde mess hall."

As they climbed the steep hill up from the mess hall after lunch the sun touched them. It filled Greta with a happiness that wanted to express itself. "Let's climb up to the meadows and see if we can spot any deer!"

"Can't. I'm going spelunking tomorrow morning." Dick shoved his hands into his pockets. There was a thoughtful look on his face. It was almost a frown.

"Again!" Greta sighed. "You'd think you'd get enough of that cold, dark old hole." She was disappointed and made no attempt to conceal the fact. "You might get lost in there. You can't go alone."

"Who says I can't? I do all the time. Besides, I know that cave like the face that stares at me from the mirror." He hesitated a bit. "Anyway, I have an idea and I have to prove it."

"Well, I don't care what you say. You might get lost. I'm going with you."

"Oh, it's better if two of us get lost? No, you can't come. You'd get lost on a vacant lot. Besides, you'd die of fright if we met up with Ghostly Gussie."

"Oh, you can't scare me off with that ridiculous talk about ghosts. I know you don't believe it any more than I do."

Dick looked at her with mock solemnity and shook his head slowly. "Don't be so sure what I believe. I know the caves a little better than you do."

"All right, guide, you can cut the dramatics. I'm no rube, you know. The play is over. I'll meet you in front of the caves at five tomorrow morning."

"I don't believe you'll be able to get out of your bed at that hour, but if you do, wear something warmer than a sweater and slacks. Something like long johns and combat boots and an arctic parka. OK? We'll be going off the beaten track and, baby, it's c-c-cold down there."

When a quarter to five came next morning, Greta rolled over to turn off her alarm clock to a chorus of groans on the sleeping porch. As she sank back into the soft bed, her resolve softened. Then, just as her mind began to blot out reality, she forced herself awake with a jerk, remembering Dick's reproachful words. She staggered out of bed and quickly pulled on her clothes, shivering in the cold, dark morning.

Now she was sitting at the side of the big opening to the hole. She was wearing her red ski underwear, jeans, stadium boots, and a couple of woolen shirts over a sweater, and she was wondering vaguely if she could even maneuver in all her gear.

The moon had not yet set, and she could see the shape of the hill where the boys' dorm sat sharply silhouetted against a gray sky. The entire resort area was quiet. There was a lonely moan of breezes in the fir trees. Just the night for a ghost, Greta thought, teasing herself. Aren't they supposed to have a particular fondness for moonlit nights? Well, they aren't any different from their living counterparts in that respect.

Then she looked up and saw a dark shape moving down the path from the boy's bunkhouse. There was Dick now, she thought, and she got up and started toward him. She had just taken a few steps when a voice from behind startled her.

"I can't believe you got here first. Women are supposed to be always late."

She whirled and saw Dick. He had come from around the hill. "I was getting a flash from the supply house."

"But I. . . ." Greta looked up the path to the bunkhouse, but the dark, moving shape was gone. "I thought I saw you coming down the trail from the bunkhouse just a minute ago."

36

"Hey, girl, get hold of yourself. We aren't even in the caves, and you're seeing things. Are you certain you want to go? We might meet Gussie, you know." His eyes were wide.

The caves were different without the tourists. They did not seem like a big show. They were real. Their footsteps down the metal railing were amplified into huge, hollow echoes by the sounding board of the cave walls.

"We'll go down as far as the Great Hall. Then I'll check out my idea."

Greta did not feel so independent with just the two of them as she had the past afternoon with the whole crowd. She stayed close to Dick and the circle of light from the flashlight that swung and bobbed and reached across the ragged floor.

"Stay here with the flashlight, will you, Greta? I'm going up on that ledge and behind that screen of columns. I've got a hunch I might find something. Just point the flash up the wall. I'll need both hands to climb."

Greta sat down on the damp ledge protruding from the wall and followed Dick's climbing form up the wall with a halo of light. After he got above the loose earth of the lower bank, he took a couple of wide-stretched steps up the rocky wall. Then he disappeared behind a curtain of iciclelike pillars. As soon as he vanished Greta felt alone. It wasn't that she was afraid. Ghosts, hah! Foolishness! But it was cold, frightfully cold, and the chill was coming

37

up from the floor and out from the walls. She stamped her feet. She glanced around the huge chamber. There on the wall across from where Dick had gone was a black, amorphous shape that flowed sinuously along the uneven surface, seemingly coming toward her. Greta gasped. The shapeless appendages were reaching . . . reaching . . . toward her. Her heart strove desperately to break through the cage of her ribs, but she made no sound. She could not scream.

"Found it. Let's go, Miss Persistent." Dick came bounding down the bank.

Greta looked up at Dick with relief, then searched the opposite wall, expecting to see the explanation of the moving shape in his shadow. But Dick's shadow was lying small and docile on the floor. With the light shining toward him his shadow would have to be behind him, not on the opposite wall.

Dick's buoyant cheerfulness made Greta feel better. She pushed the specter or whatever it was to the back of her mind as well as she could. But even as she heard Dick's enthusiastic voice, the thing hovered in her subconscious and she became more and more tense.

Getting down on their hands and knees, they wriggled into the opening that Dick had located behind the pillars. Greta followed behind Dick as she pulled herself along on her stomach under the hanging knobs of limestone formations. The floor was wet and muddy. Greta pushed and squirmed toward Dick and his light. Then suddenly the passageway opened wide, and there was a fantastically beautiful, high-ceilinged chamber before them.

"Look! We discovered it ourselves. It isn't shown on any map of the caves." Dick was jubilant.

The cavern seemed to be filled with an exotic garden of limestone formations, growing lushly from floor and ceiling. Some were fluted and ridged elaborately. Some were bulbous. Some were streaked red from the iron in the limestone, like bloodstained mushrooms. There were golden yellow columns that shaded and faded into smooth, translucent white, reflecting the light damply, glossily.

Greta stared in dumb admiration, not knowing how to express the overwhelming awe in her. It was like finding a globe of crystallized eternity. Everything was so untouched, so pure, a secret treasure deposited by the ages. Time did not seem to exist in this motionless place. Then a drop of cold water fell on Greta's head. She looked up to see another drop swelling on a low-hanging orange stalactite, reminding her that time and motion had penetrated even here.

"Dick, it's the loveliest chamber in the caves! Don't tell anyone about it."

"Kind of reminds me of something I read about the dark flowers that bloom in the mysterious caverns of the soul."

Greta was surprised. She hadn't thought him capable of saying something like that. "Let's not tell anyone about it, Dick. It would be ruined if we turned it over to the rubes. There'd be bubble gum stuck all over the formations and 'Joe was here' scratched on the walls."

Greta turned to Dick, feeling suddenly earnest and intense, just in time to see his face fading into blackness. The light of the flash grew weaker, then brighter, then wavered until she could see the white incandescence of the filament outlined by its blue halo. It flared once more before her horrified eyes, then died into blackness.

"Dick! What happened, what happened?"

"I . . . don't know. Maybe the batteries. I've been using this flash quite a while. What a dopey thing not to bring batteries. . . ."

Greta shivered. The beautiful world of a minute ago had been blotted out completely. She couldn't help thinking of the shadow in the Great Hall, and as she shuddered the whole cavern seemed filled with the same all-devouring shadow, swathing them in its dark cloak. She wanted to tell Dick about the shadow, but forming the words would make it more real, so in her subconscious the ghost of Augusta Guthrie grew ever larger, more palpable. She strove to keep it from being conscious. As long as Dick was not afraid, she could borrow from his strength.

"What'll we do, Dick? Can we feel our way back?"

40

"We'd better be able to. We're so far back now no one would ever hear us yell. Greta, here, hold my hand. We can't get separated in here; we'd be sunk. . . . Hey! I've got a couple of matches."

Dick struck one of the matches and illumined the chamber. They looked around for their entrance. The formations had a strange sameness. They were too unfamiliar. There were no landmarks they could use. Dick struck another match when the first had burned his fingers. Then, in the light of the third match, they saw an opening.

"Come on." Dick was feeling his way toward the opening. "If we can get to the Great Hall, I know where there's a supply of batteries near the steps up to the Cathedral. Here's the opening." Dick's voice was filled with relief.

Greta held tightly to his hand as he worked his feet down through the opening.

"Hey!" he yelled. "Hey! This isn't. . . ."

As soon as he spoke the pull on Greta's hand became too strong. He slipped from her grasp and was gone. "Dick! Dick! What happened? Where are you? Are you in the Great Hall?"

There was no sound from Dick. Greta felt choked. The skin over her entire body prickled with new sensitivity. She could feel the flow of cold air currents she had not noticed before. She had only one thought—to find Dick. He might have been hurt!

Greta pushed her legs down into the hole, hung

on to the edge as long as she could, then. . . . *"Eeeeeeeeeeh."* She screamed as she began sliding down a steep, muddy bank.

"Dick! Dick!" Her voice was tremulous. She had stopped sliding, but the darkness prevented her from seeing what kind of a place it was. "Please, Dick, please. Where are you?" It was as dark in this pit as in the one above, but she knew it was not the Great Hall. That much she could tell by a sixth sense. They were working farther and farther into the cave . . . into the mountain.

Then Greta heard it. It was a high-pitched note. She listened closely. It could not be Dick. No human being living could make a sound like that. The word *living* had popped uninvited into her mind, and how she wished it hadn't. She leaned against the muddy bank in the total oblivion and heard the high-pitched shriek with helpless terror.

She felt about her. The cave was large. She could stand up. She started staggering around, walking, now half jogging over the uneven floor, blindly, almost hysterically. As she walked, something brushed her. Something moving, which scratched her face clawlike and brushed by with a floating motion. Greta wanted to cry out, but her throat was closed tight. It was like a nightmare. She was trying to get somewhere and she could not get there, and she wanted to scream and she couldn't. She slowed down and held her hands ahead of her. The cavern was narrowing. It was a cold light, without warmth, and it silhouetted a many-tentacled, moving shape, pulsating, flowing, growing, shrinking slowly . . . slowly.

It is! It is! The ghost of Augusta Guthrie! Greta could see the fluttering sunbonnet strings, the slowly billowing skirt, even . . . even . . . the glowing, empty eyes.

Greta's hand flew to her mouth. She bit her lip in anguish and terror. She moved slowly backward, unable to turn her face away from the apparition that was reaching toward her . . . reaching . . . reaching.

As she backed along, the passageway grew smaller, and she inched along the wall, which turned suddenly. "Oh!" Greta gasped with disbelief at what she saw. It was a shaft of light. A thin, warm, oblique, sun-born band, dancing with myriad dust motes suspended within it like an infinitesimal milky way. "Oh!" Greta repeated, and the relief she felt reached through her body and loosened the fear.

She raced forward wildly to the ray of light. She found a small opening as she searched the rocks. It had a well-worn pathway with small footprints of what appeared to be a raccoon. It was surprisingly easy to work her way out of the opening, which was covered thickly with mountain laurel. She worked through the bushes, scratching herself as she went. Then she glanced around quickly to see where she was. She was on the other side of the crest from the opening, on the low side of the bank. That's how there could be an opening to the surface even though they had gone deeper. She ran around the side of the hill as rapidly as she could and got a flashlight from the guide's shack near the mouth of the cave. In the early-morning light she did not think of the ghost, but as she again approached the opening she felt the fear swell within her. Pushing aside the bushes, she entered the same way she had come out. She hoped that the apparition had gone to other quarters, because she did not know if she had courage to face it again. But she had to find Dick.

"Dick! Dick!" she cupped her hands to her mouth as she called. Then she heard a stumbling sound.

"Greta, I'm here. I'm coming."

Forgetting about the apparition in her relief at hearing Dick's voice, she ran forward and then she saw it. An old piece of cloth hanging from a hole in the wall, fluttering with the breeze from the passageway to the outside. But the glow?

As she rounded the turn she saw Dick. He came down the corridor with a slight limp, but with a smile spread all over his face.

"Boy, am I glad to see you. That darned phosphorous deposit with that old rag flapping over it gave me quite a start. Some raccoon or something put it in that hole, I'll bet. There's a lot of other junk from the trash barrels too, and look at all the animal tracks around it."

Greta led him quickly to the opening, and his eyes lit up as though he were seeing a Christmas tree full of presents.

"Say . . . good girl! This is something we can't keep secret. The Park Service hasn't the slightest idea there's another way out of the caves."

"Let's tell them the whole thing." Greta's face glowed as she spoke. "It would be selfish not to let other people see that room you discovered. Let's call it the Chamber of Dark Flowers, OK?"

Dick grinned his acquiescence as though he appreciated her selection.

At last, scratched but happy, they were sitting on the ground outside the cave. The sun was coming over the horizon, evaporating the last residue of fear and giving courage with its golden touch.

"I've got to hand it to you, Greta. You've got what it takes."

"How do you mean? Finding the opening?"

"Yeah, that too. But I mean you never once panicked about that ghost or anything. Cool as a hunk of ice all the way. Man, when I made that hand shadow on the cavern wall by holding my hand in front of a match, I darn near scared myself, it looked so bad. When a bat flew into me later, I nearly jumped out of my hide."

"Bat!" Greta grimaced and her hands flew up to her face.

"That's what I said. Didn't you know there were

bats in the caves? Couldn't you hear that high-pitched squeak?"

"Oh, no!" Greta twisted her mouth in disgust. "I'm glad I didn't know. Ghosts are one thing, but bats . . . boy!"

"You are crazy, Greta. Crazy, crazy!" Dick grabbed her hand as they started trotting down the hill "Hang on tight so you won't get lost," he said.

As they came closer to the clearing, Greta glanced up the path to the boys' dormitory and saw it, or at least another one just like it. It was the shape she had seen before in the darkness. It was a doe, still black in the early dawn. It stood, hesitating a moment, then leaped into the brush beside the trail. "Oh, look!" Greta was breathless. "That's what it was. When I was waiting for you this morning, I thought you were a deer . . . or . . . I . . . I mean. . . ."

Dick started laughing. "Gee, thanks. I think you're pretty nice yourself."

"Oh, cut it out, Dick." Greta was embarrassed. "You know. . . ."

But he was pulling her into a jogging run down the twisting path. Then they were running faster and faster, and laughing harder and harder, as they neared the resort clearing below where the first smoke of the day rose thinly on the air.

The Problem Solver
and the Spy

CHRISTOPHER ANVIL

Richard Verner leaned back in his office chair with the alert look of a big cat as across the desk Nathan Bancroft, a quietly dressed man of average height, spoke earnestly.

"Last Saturday, Mr. Verner, a technician at one of our most highly classified research laboratories got away with the plans for a new and secret type of laser device. The scientist who invented the device evidently tried to stop him and was stabbed to death."

Verner nodded intently.

Bancroft went on. "To understand the situation

47

that's come about, you have to know that the region around this laboratory has a great many caverns. They are connected in a gigantic system of natural tunnels, rooms, crevices, and underground streams that have never been thoroughly mapped or explored.

"The technologist who stole the plans is an ardent speleologist—a cave explorer. Possibly one reason for his hobby is that he suffers from hay fever, and cavern air is pure. In any case, over a period of years he's spent entire days in an underground complex of branching tunnels known as the Maze of Minos. A number of cave explorers have been lost in there, and the local people shun it. The only known expert on this underground maze is the murderer himself.

"Now there's no question, Mr. Verner, but that this spy expected to be far away before the theft of the plans was discovered. But, by sheer good luck, the director of the laboratory discovered what had happened and immediately notified the police. The police were lucky too; they spotted the technician's car just after the call came in. But then we all ran out of luck. The technician, taking the plans with him, escaped into this cavern, this Maze of Minos."

"And got away?" said Verner.

"Got clean away," said Bancroft. "The tunnels branch off in all directions, and, of course, it's as dark in there as the blackest night. He simply vanished."

Verner nodded again. "He's still

Bancroft said glumly, "Yes, he's s
have a great many men on the spot
but watching the known exits. But
the chance that he'll find some ne
knows of one, and get away. Meanwime, we desperately need those plans. With the inventor dead, there
are certain details we can clear up only from those
papers. Yet, if we should get close, he might take
it into his head to destroy them. What we want to
do is to get to him before he realizes we're near.
But how? How do we even *find* him in there?"

"Is he starving?"

"Not likely. He probably has caches of food for
his longer explorations. And there's water in the
caverns, if you know where to look."

"You want to get him alive and by surprise?"

"Exactly."

"But he knows you're hunting for him in the cavern?"

"Oh, yes. We've brought in light, and before we
realized what we were up against, we set up loud-
speakers and warned him to give up or we'd come
in after him. If he understood what we were saying
over all the echoes, this must have amused him immensely. We could put our whole organization in
there and get nothing out of a grand-scale search
but sore feet, chills, and a few dozen men lost in
the winding passages. The thing is a standoff, and he
knows it."

Verner asked thoughtfully, "And what brings you to me?"

Bancroft smiled. "We've consulted cave explorers, geologists, and all kinds of specialists without finding what we want. Then one of our men, who knows General Granger, remembered his saying he'd been helped in that mess at the hunting lodge by a heuristician. We got in touch with Granger, who recommended you highly. We didn't know exactly what heuristician was, but we're prepared to try anything."

Verner laughed. "A heuristician is a professional problem solver. I work on the assumption that nearly all problems can be solved by the same basic technique combined with expert knowledge. Some of my cases are scientific, some involve business situations, and others are purely personal problems. The details vary, but the basic technique remains the same. If the case interests me enough to take it in the first place, and if the necessary expert help is available, I can usually solve any problem, though sometimes there's an unavoidable element of luck and uncertainty."

"Well," said Bancroft, "we have plenty of experts on hand—all kinds. And I hope this problem offers enough of a challenge to interest you."

Verner nodded. "And we'd better lose no time getting there."

Many cars and big trucks were parked outside

the main cavern entrance. From outside, electric cables coiled into the brilliantly lighted mouth of the cavern, and there was a steady throb of engines as Verner and Bancroft walked in.

"Generators," said Bancroft. "We're trying to light this end as brightly as possible and extend the lights inward. But it's a hopeless job. I'll show you why."

They pushed past a small crowd of men, who nodded to Bancroft and glanced at Verner curiously, and then they were in a brightly lighted chamber in the rock, about forty feet long by ten high, and twelve to fourteen feet wide. Here their voices and footsteps echoed as Bancroft led the way toward the far end, where a faint breeze of cool air blew in their faces.

"So far, so good," said Bancroft, stepping around a tangle of cables and walking through a narrow doorway cut in the rock. "But here we begin to run into trouble."

He stepped back to show a long, brightly lit chamber where fantastic friezelike shapes dipped from the ceiling to meet fairy castles and miniature ranges of mountains rising from the floor. Here the electric cables that lay along the floor fanned out in all directions, to wind around huge pointed cones into the well-lighted distance.

Wherever Verner looked, the stalactites and stalagmites rose and dipped endlessly, with new chambers opening out in different directions, and as Bancroft led the way they clambered over the uneven, slanting floor past waterfalls of rock, through little grottoes, and by shapes like thrones, statues, and weird creatures from fairyland.

For a long time they walked in silence except for the echoes of their own footsteps. Then suddenly it was dark ahead. The last giant electric bulb lit the shapes of stalagmites rising, one behind the other, till the farthest ones were lost in impenetrable shadows.

A gentle breeze was still in their faces—cool, refreshing, and pure. Somewhere ahead of them they could hear a faint trickling of water.

"Here," said Bancroft, "we come to the end of our string. These tunnels branch, then open out into rooms, and the rooms have galleries leading off from them, and out of these galleries there are still more tunnels. They twist, wind, and occasionally they even rejoin."

His voice echoed as he talked, and he pointed off to the right. "Over there, somewhere—I think that's the direction—there's an eighty-foot sheer drop with a little stream at the bottom, and from the wall of this drop other tunnels open out in various directions and on different levels. There are eyeless fish in the stream, and a kind of blind salamander. Very interesting, but our problem is the complex of all those tunnels. A man who knew where he was going could pick the one tunnel he wanted out of a dozen or so at any given place. But we have to follow them all, and every so often they divide again or—look up there."

Bancroft pointed to a dark opening above a slope like a frozen waterfall. "Probably that's another one. This whole place is honeycombed, filled with diverging and connecting tunnels. It's like trying to track down someone inside a man-size termite's nest. We thought he might have left some trace, some sign of where he'd gone. We thought we could follow him with dogs. We forgot that he's practically lived in here during his spare time ever since the laboratory was set up.

"There's a superabundance of clues. Dogs have followed one track through the dark, right over the edge of a sudden drop, and been killed. We can find signs that he's been just about anywhere we look. We found a pair of sneakers at one place and a cache of food at another." Bancroft shook his head. "Let's go out. There are some people you'll want to meet now that you've seen what it's like in here, what our problem is."

Outside, in the warm fall night, a group of men quickly gathered around Verner and Bancroft. One, an old man in dungarees and checked shirt, was well known locally as a cave explorer. A tall man in a gray business suit was the director of the government laboratory, and he repeatedly sneezed and blew his nose. A boy in dungarees and old leather jacket told how he had seen the murderer-spy enter the cave after crossing a nearby field; he was sure it was the man they were looking for.

"We all knew him. We'd often see him go in here. He knows more about these caves than anyone—well, except maybe Gramp Peters here."

The old man laughed. "Don't fool yourself. I know old Minotaur, at the other end of this, like I know the back of my hand. But the Maze—I admit I don't know it. I was in here maybe ten years ago, got lost, wandered around for five days, drinking the water in an underground stream, and finally made my way out of a collapsed sinkhole miles away from here. That was the end of the Maze for me. Now this man you're looking for is a different animal. He's as good as lived in there."

The laboratory director sneezed and blew his nose again. "One reason he spent so much time there, especially in the fall, was the pure air of the caverns. He was, if anything, even more allergic than I am. He once told me that the only place an active man could find recreation out of doors in the fall, if he suffered from hay fever, was inside a cave."

Bancroft said, "We're watching all the known exits. We've sent teams of men through those tunnels, and we've only begun to grasp the difficulties. Somehow we've *got* to locate him—but how?"

Verner glanced at the old man. "There seems to be a slight, steady current of air in there. That doesn't come from the outside, does it?"

Gramp Peters shook his head. "These passages are complicated, but in this part of the cavern most of the passages slope a little uphill. Up at the other end is what they call the Minotaur. There's an underground riverbed there—no river, that's eaten its way farther down—but there's this gentle flow of cold air. I suppose the air comes from the outside somewhere, maybe from hundreds of miles away, but you wouldn't know it by the time it gets here. It seems to flow into the Minotaur and then branch out through the Maze. It's always fresh and cool. If you get turned around in a passage, that gentle breeze, when you come to a narrow place, will tell you which way you're headed."

When Verner was finished asking questions, Bancraft took him aside. "You see now what we're up against, Mr. Verner?"

"I suppose you've got infrared equipment?"

"Yes, and if we knew where he was, it might help us find our way to him in the dark without warning him. But it won't help to send teams of men prospecting at random through all those tunnels. The last time we tried it we found nothing, and three men were seriously injured when they came to a sudden slope." He looked at Verner tensely. "Do you have *any* suggestion, any idea at all?"

Verner nodded. "If we're lucky, and if what we've been told is true, we *may* have him out of there in a few hours."

"If you can do that, you're a miracle worker."

"No miracle at all, just common sense. But this is a case where we'll need a little luck. And we'll have to work from the upper end, from the Minotaur."

The passages of the Minotaur were larger and looked less complicated than those in the Maze. Here the gentle current of cool air seemed stronger, steadier, and could sometimes be felt even in comparatively wide passages.

Verner and Bancroft waited tensely, and then down the passage ahead came a small group, carrying a struggling man who was swearing violently.

"*Find* him?" said one of his captors, grinning. "All we had to do was follow the sounds he was making. He was sitting by a cache of food that would have lasted a week, with the plans still in his pocket."

Bancroft was looking at Verner, but he didn't speak. An awful choking and strangling from the prisoner made Bancroft turn in amazement. The choking and strangling noises were interspersed with violent sneezing.

Down the passage the men had stopped thrashing the stacks of ragweed, which had sent thick clouds of pollen drifting through the passage and into the Maze. The pollen had unerringly found its target— the murderer-thief who suffered from hay fever.

Lost in the Caverns

WILLIAM LINDSAY GRESHAM

Standing with both shoulders in line with a sycamore trunk, Ian rested the stock of his long rifle on one moccasin toe and waited. Beneath his feet he could feel the ghostly murmur of a river underground—witch water carving its secret channels where the sun had never shone.

Horses were entering the gorge. There were voices and the ring of an iron shoe on rock. When they filed into view, he saw that Judge Rainey came first on a big bay, wearing his old cocked hat; the judge had fought in the War of Independence and was proud of it. After him rode Miles Winter, the store-keeper down at the settlement. And then came a young woman, a stranger. She sat slender and straight on the judge's little gray mare.

Ian left the cover of the tree and crept down the ravine side to a ledge just above them, where he lay flat, listening to their talk.

". . . only way to fetch him is to build a fire and smudge it. We'll make a smoke, ma'am, and cut it back and forth with a saddle blanket. Then we'll wait." Judge Rainey's rumble.

The girl spoke. "How far will this man have to come? How do you know he will come? How do you know he'll help us? Oh, show me the way in, and I'll take a light and go after the child myself."

"Now then, Mis' Lorimer, you been bearin' up till now," Miles Winter put in soothingly. "Ain't any of us going into that place long as Ian Farr's in the country. Why, ma'am, inside there you'd be lost afore you could turn 'round. Farr's own wife got lost in there, hiding from a Shawnee raid, twenty years back. Some say he never did find her; say he spent a year and more, threadin' in and out of them caverns, and nary a trace of her."

That was when Ian rose, looking down at them from the ledge. His voice was hollow and slow, the voice of a forest man. "If'n the woman has lost a young un, why don't her own man hunt it?"

They were startled. The woodsman's eyes were smoky in a mahogany face. His hair was cut roughly with a hunting knife, the same knife that had skinned a deer to provide him with his shirt. He was a man of the deep woods, and now he stood silent, waiting for them to speak.

The young woman said, "You are Mr. Farr, I suppose. My name is Esther Lorimer. My little daughter is lost. Mr. Winter's dogs tracked her this far. The trail ended . . . at a fissure in the rock." Her eyes were dark and her hair was tawny. Upon her finger was a gold band.

"Where is your man?" Ian asked.

She sat a little straighter. "My husband is dead."

The judge said, "Captain Lorimer died last winter, time Luke Felton's team went through the ice. He was helping get 'em out. Caught a chill and died. Now come down off'n that perch, Ian Farr, and help this woman find her girl. If the child's in that devil's hole, you're the man to fetch her out."

Ian leaped lightly the seven feet from the ledge to the ravine moss. When Esther Lorimer saw him at close range, her heart quickened, for in truth he did look like a savage. There was no insolence in his stare; it was the curiosity of a wild thing.

She said softly, "I should be forever in your debt, Mr. Farr."

The woodsman said nothing. Miles Winter had unstrapped his saddlebags and was taking out candles and a lantern with a glass window. These Ian picked up without asking leave and dropped into a vast pocket on the left side of his shirt. He lifted a coil of braided rawhide rope from the judge's saddle horn, again without asking, and thrust his arm through it, hanging it from his shoulder. Then he let his eyes flick over the three of them and settle on the woman. He held out the slim-barreled flintlock. "Hit's got a load in it."

He knew she was no immigrant, just fresh come over the Wilderness Road, by the way she cradled the rifle in the crook of her arm, its muzzle sloping toward the sky; her fingers about the trigger guard were slender and strong. He hated her for a wild moment until he recalled that her man was dead. After that he did not look at her again.

Kneeling to blow on smoldering tinder between his cupped hands, flint and steel beside him, he asked, "What's your girl's name?"

"Martha. She is just turned seven years, Mr. Farr."

Daylight flickered down into the ravine through laurel branches; the candle in the lantern seemed to have no flame. Ian hung it from a brown finger and turned toward the rock wall, parting the vines.

There, before him, was his old enemy, the cleft of darkness, a gash in the stone: Farr's Cave. He reached in as if trying to grip a handful of dark. Then he ducked his head and vanished.

Eighteen years since Ian had set foot in the caverns he had discovered. More days than Cora had been on earth, time they were wed. It had dulled over finally, all of it—the remembrance of Cora in daybreak light, standing white and slim, putting up her hair. Remembrance of the last night, the raid, the flight to the caverns, his return, after scouting, to find her gone; and then the frenzied search of aisles, crypts, and passages, dreading what he might find, yet driven on to find it.

He never found it. The years went rolling over, with Ian hunting and fishing farther to the west, setting snares and deadfalls, taking pelts, kneeling sometimes the space of an hour, listening to the silence of deep woods or the distant scolding of a jay. Witch water, born in darkness underground and never healed by the sun, would set a man apart, some said; a man who drank witch water was forest-bound for life, restless under a roof. Well, he'd drunk it, drowned in it, pretty near, searching Inkhorn Lake for Cora's body.

And the witch water of the caves had worked on him in the end. For many seasons he had not heard Cora's name spoken, but it remained a canker in his heart. Then one April day when freshets thundered from a sudden rain, he recollected he had not even thought of Cora since the spring before. When a signal smoke in the ravine brought him to trade furs for gunpowder with men from the settlement, her name was never mentioned. They had forgot it, likely. New faces coming in all the time, the great valley flattening into fields, and children straying far in their play, with no fear of Shawnee war cries anymore.

Ian picked his way over the passage floor. Stooping, he entered another chamber, and in the candle

61

gleam on limestone saw in a niche a twig with a mile of fishline wound on it in a great black bulge, undisturbed since he had flung it there, long time ago. He wouldn't need it again. It had served during the first months, guiding him back, but now he knew the caverns as once he had known the soft shadows of Cora's face.

For a week he had shouted her name, until his voice cracked into a whisper. Cora. Cora. Cora. And never an answer above the distant roar of Inkhorn Lake, plunging into darkness, and the closer drip of water with its many voices.

Suddenly he shouted, "Cora!" and the sound came falling back upon him. But the little lost girl was named Martha, her mother waiting outside.

He tried again. "Martha! Martha Lorimer!"

Only the drip of water answered, same as it had times long ago. He tried to think of what a settlement child would do, wandering in the caves. But about white children he knew little, except Cora's dreaming aloud.

Ian lying quiet in wordless delight, and Cora whispering the future. "Ian, it would pleasure me if you'd make me a cradle. And I could make a doll for it, just to rock while we're waiting. A cradle would be a gladsome thing by the hearth . . . and having the doll, I'd sew little gowns for it."

Afterward Ian found her sewing scissors, black among the still-fuming ashes of the house. He had scaled them into the weeds before thinking that some settlement woman would treasure them. To him they were blades driven in the heart.

Fighting off the past, the woodsman raised his lantern. Ahead curved the glistening sheet of flowstone, beyond which lay the first of the great caverns. When he laid his hand upon the flowstone, he marveled again that it could be so hard, while seeming as if you could push your fingers into it. . . .

That night they had not bothered to stop for it; they had not stopped to marvel at anything. Softly that night was treading in upon him, memory by memory, remorseless as the water drip on stone.

. . . a glow in the sky above the ridge, saddling Toby while Cora held the light, wind sweeping sparks high, from the ridge a sight of the Williams' cabin burning, roar of a rifle inside, door flung back, Evan Williams hurtling out with his shirt flaming and a Shawnee arrow appearing in his side, Williams plucking at it while two more seemed to sprout from his back. Ian never waited to see him fall.

Wheeling Toby and racing down the wood road, leaning low on the horse's neck to dodge branches, Cora's arms around his neck as Toby plunged on in the darkness. The mouth of the gorge. Unbridling, cutting the girth, slap of reins on Toby's flanks driving him back, continuing on foot. Cora's breath failing as she pleaded, "Oh, Ian, let's rest."

He gathered her up in his arms, turning once to

watch the scarlet glow above their own place, but Cora was precious and warm, safe with him if they could reach the hidden mouth of the caverns.

They reached it, parting the vines. Then groping for the tinderbox he had stored there, candles safe from mice in an old tea canister, the light leaping, and Cora's gasp at the brilliance of the jeweled walls.

"You wait, Cora. Hit's provisioned a ways in. Smoked venison haunches, bearskins for a bed, gourd dipper. We'll drink witch water out of Inkhorn Lake."

Ian had prepared their refuge, foreseeing their needs. They would not starve; they would not thirst. But he had not foreseen fear. . . .

The gaunt man in grease-blackened buckskin shook his head to rid it of memory. Again he called, "Martha! Martha Lorimer! Your ma's waiting!"

Stone pillars and walls answered him, ". . . waiting . . . waiting."

The passage narrowed. Here was the place where Cora caught her skirt and stumbled against him. Here they kissed as if they were sparking, instead of a respectable couple a year wed.

He stepped out into a vault so vast that the shine from his lantern was swallowed up. Here was a cathedral worn by a buried river. As a boy he had brought in firewood and by its blaze had seen the mighty arch of the roof with the seam drip fringing it like festoons of stone hair. That was before ever Cora had come to the settlement, when he had gone venturing into the caves just to wonder and to find out where they led.

The floor was smooth for a way, then steps of stone, and at last he came to the far end and the pile of boulders. Ian cast his light about and called again, sure that no child could climb that crazed pile of rock. Then he recalled a narrow way beneath them, too perilous slim for any but a child.

Ian started to climb. Somewhere in this labyrinth of water-worn stone the Lorimer girl might be lying, injured, crazed with fear, lost, crying out for her mother in the darkness. Just as Cora must have cried out his own name . . . and then the long-buried panic welled up in him again, destroying the peace of his forest years.

When he called, his voice was higher pitched. "Martha! This here's a neighbor! Martha!"

From far ahead he heard, louder now, the roar of water tumbling over rocks. The child could not be behind him; the first branching passage was past this boulder pile. Crushing down his own horror, he climbed again, feeling for remembered footholds.

At the top of the madly slanting heap he lifted his light. The child, if she had the sense of forest children, would stay put and holler every now and then like a screech owl or bark like a fox. But a settlement child would likely run here and yonder in the dark and dash her head against a low ceiling.

Making fast the rawhide line, he slid down the far side of the pile, gripping with his toes through moccasin soles. At the bottom was a smooth dip of rock shelf, which he had named the Hammock. Cora had rested for a moment here, spreading her skirt on the stone, his arm about her.

He had nestled close, feeling her lips on his hair. His voice muffled as she held him, he said comfortingly, "Our place is a hidey-hole up a ways, through a narrow notch. It's by the lake—water black as the ink in an inkhorn. I named it Inkhorn Lake when I was a young un. If'n you hear something trouble the water, don't frighten at hit, Cora. There's little fish in there, moon white and blind. There's fish, Cora, honey. We'll go a-fishing while . . . while the painted folks is a-looking for us outside." He was talking to reassure her. She knew it, and instead of words she gave him her mouth upon his, familiar after a year's life together, yet kindling to something wild-sweet, with doom and destruction left behind them under the blazing night. Here there were just the two of them, lovers, like courtship times.

Ian Farr turned from the Hammock, letting out his breath in a rebellious sob at the thrust of memory. "You still got to slide through the notch," he told himself. "You ain't found the girl nor any sign of her."

The lantern showed a tilted passage, sharp rising; at its end the walls folded toward a narrow, triangular hole. He set the light in a niche where he could reach back and get it. Then on hands and knees, he pushed himself into the notch.

What if the stone had shifted, closing in a mite since last he snaked his way through here? It was always a squeeze for him, but Cora, clinging to his hands, had been drawn through easy enough.

Limestone ground his cheek as he inched forward, toes slipping on the passage floor behind him. Another inch. A finger's breadth more. Wait . . . the notch had grown smaller! It must have. There was a foot more of it, and now, groping, he got the old, remembered handgrip again and hauled and made no progress. His chest was stuck; his head felt flattened. Then panic, such as he had never known his life long, poured scalding in upon him, and he began to thresh with his legs, frantic to free himself from this trap of stone like a man caught in his own deadfall set for bear.

At last, panting and clammy, he felt the limestone grate under him. He fell back into the passage, his breath whistling. In its niche the light began to flicker, and Ian took a fresh candle from his pocket, picked open the hot metal door of the lantern, and replenished his light. He began to think again. Likely the stones had not moved; likely he had growed. He was twenty-two when Cora . . . vanished. And a man's shoulders and chest keep growing, especially toting deer into camp over steep ridges. Young Ian Farr could get through that crevice. But Ian Farr, growed big. . . .

A child could slip through there like a mouse through a fox den.

Cautiously Ian slid into it again, until he felt the jaws grip him. He filled his lungs and shouted, just for luck, "Martha Lorimer! Air ye in there? Your ma's a-waiting on ye! Martha!"

He let his jaw drop, like an Indian straining to listen. Anywhere the child might be, it would be within sound of his voice, likely. Better to call for a spell and keep calling, holding the lantern in the notch so's she could see the glimmer and come toward it . . . if'n she weren't hurt or too scairt to holler.

He tried again. "Martha! Martha Lorimer! I've come to fetch you home!"

Then he remembered. By the lake's ledge the roar of water, diving into the earth somewhere at the other end of the cavern, would drown his voice. Best to go back, get a party of men from the settlement with crowbars and picks, and take a chance on widening the notch.

For an instant, in the black triangle ahead of him, he thought he could make out a faint flicker of light. Shielding the lantern, he closed his eyes, rested them, and opened them toward the darkness. Something had winked and glittered in there, far in by the lake. A candle, hid from sight, would reflect that sort of gleam. And if the child had come this far, she might stray into side galleries on her way back.

If only he had known Farr's Cave, with all its traps and mazes, when Cora vanished into it as well as he knew it now.

Then, as he watched, a stalactite glowed dimly and faded into the pitch night of the cavern. The Lorimer child, searching for a way back, likely. And no good to call her from here.

Ian seized the buckskin hunting shirt, drew it over his head, dropping it to the floor. His undervest of soft fawn came next. Naked to the waist, he crouched at the opening, drew three deep, whistling breaths, and let out the last one until all the air was gone from him. Then he hurled his shoulders at the crevice, scrabbling with moccasined toes, pushing, grinding his cheek against limestone that seemed so smooth to the sight and was like a file rasping at his flesh. He stuck.

Groping ahead, he reached the handhold again, then drew up one knee and found a dent in the wall with his foot. His back and chest took fire, his ribs bent, but the sweat that made his fingers slippery helped him where it ran down his sides. Death did not pursue him here; death waited here, lingering and nightmarish. No blazing Shawnee death, but death cold, death black, death taking its time.

Ian's skull seemed crushed; where his hair caught, needles seemed to drive into his scalp. Once beyond, he would not die of thirst at least, and hunger is no fearsome death, but here—

All the stored fear and desperation of the old search flooded back, its poison doubled by its long burial in the mind.

Gasping, he heard the sweating skin of his belly

69

slap the rock, sound like a fish landed, fighting for breath on the shore. In a snarling rage he fought the trap jaws, tearing his moccasins loose. Breathing through his teeth, he fought the very earth itself, one raging, clawing life spark against the eternal stone.

He gained an inch, tearing and crushing himself toward freedom. Another. And now the rock was slippery, as it had never been without his blood. A last, violent wrench and his head and chest emerged. He wriggled, helping with his elbows; his hips cleared and he slumped forward, gulping air again. The hot sting of air on his torn flesh seemed sweet and upholding. When he could sit up, he reached back through the notch and lifted out the lantern.

A passage ahead and more piled fragments from an old cave-in, so ancient that the rocks were mortared together with limestone flow. Then at last he stood on the precipice. In the pool of lantern light lay an expanse of water, death quiet, shining black, while from far across it, through the perpetual night, came the boom of the outlet, a different note than he remembered it.

He cupped his hand beside his lips and shouted for the last time, "Martha!"

To his left, hidden from sight beneath a sheer drop of stone, light struck out, winking a patch across the surface of the lake, and a small voice cried, "Hel-lo-o-o! I'm down here!"

His lantern clinking against jutting fingers of rock, the woodsman scrambled down toward the hidden source of sound and candle shine. But something was wrong—the lake had sunk itself, the bank was never this deep! He came to a plateau like a table, which had not been there before. And from a lower gallery, strange to him, the light shone, silhouetting a slight form in a singlet of homespun.

When Ian stepped close, the child jumped to her feet, her eyes round at the specter of a half-naked man whose chest was a raw wound.

"My name's Farr, ma'am," he said hoarsely. "Your ma sent me a-looking for you."

"Oh." She seemed less skittish now, taking in his torn leggings, his moccasins, his milk-white shoulders, and brown face. "Oh, you fell and got hurt. I'm sorry. Let me wash you off some."

"It's nothing, ma'am. A little b'ar grease'll fix hit."

The child's eyes settled on his own, not in fear this time, but in some odd regret. "If you're Mr. Farr, this must be your cave. I—I didn't know you'd be angered at me . . . playing in your cave, Mr. Farr."

Ian knelt swiftly. "Nor am I, ma'am. I ain't . . . I ain't used it in quite a spell. Only you mought git lost in hit. I come to fetch you home."

Martha Lorimer sat down with dignity, guarding the flame of her candle with her hand. She said, looking up at him, "Some tell as how you're daft, Mr. Farr, living in the woods so long. But Ma says not to believe a body that speaks ill of another."

Beyond them, far out in the pitch night, there was a splash, faint and ghostly, as a fish leaped. Ian

71

shifted his lantern. "Don't them splashes frighten you, young un?"

"Only at first they did. Then I guessed they were fish. Fish sound the same up above, in the creek near home. But the first times I was a bit scared."

The hunter leaped to his feet. "You mean you been in here afore?"

Martha nodded. "I used up all the candles I found in an old box. Then I brought more. I didn't mean to stay so long this time. I should have gone back before Ma worried. Only I found a new place this time. It's off that way. I found a lady in it. She was smiling at me."

Ian froze, his breath still. Sweat, salty and cold, touched the corners of his mouth. When he could speak, his tongue was thick; his hand shook as he picked up the lantern. "Show me to that place, young un."

Guarding the candle stub with her hand, the child stepped agilely along the rock ledge, climbing without effort, as graceful as a squirrel. The man followed. His breath came short and his mouth was cottony.

Above his head a line showed where the lake surface had been. Inkhorn Lake must have worn away boulders in its drop deeper into the earth until one day the barrier cut loose and raging water fought through, the lake sinking to its present level. The contours of the cavern wall were different entirely seen from this angle. Ian was seized with a gripping strangeness; this was new country now, only a man's height below the lakeshore that he knew.

Martha Lorimer said, squirming up to another ledge, "There's a cave room up the bank a ways with things in it. But all I could make out for sure was a dipper. There are things covered with green dust. I guess they were a bed of skins once. Somebody lived in here. I guess it was the lady."

The path sloped down; the child ducked under an overhanging claw of stone. Ian paused, tightened his jaw muscles, and followed.

They stood in a gleaming, jeweled grotto, which in his day had been below water. Even his frenzied diving and groping along the rock walls had never revealed a hint of it. But he remembered a slow current that drove in against this edge of the lake and seemed to suck downward.

The child stepped aside, holding her flickering flame. "See," she whispered. "There's the smiling lady."

It lay on its side, a ghostly web, which had been a dress of homespun, making a dark smudge around the bones. They were tiny bones, picked clean by time and the waters under the earth. A wonder they were still together. The delicate skull lay on its side with the jaw in place, and it smiled in the candle shine.

Ian dropped to his knees. It was the end of the journey. And no heartbreak or horror in it anywhere. It was simply death, and by now death was an old companion. Cora seemed to smile at him across a great chasm of time. Gently he touched the smooth jaw with his finger, remembering Cora's face —the broad brow, the curve of cheek, the little elfish chin, determined enough when they were together, but trembling oftentimes when she was not by his side. She was no girl to face the wilderness nor ever should have come up the Wilderness Road.

Martha's voice broke his reverie. "Some people are afraid of skeletons. But Ma says they are just houses with the people moved away."

His mouth was dry no longer. He said, wondering at the blurring of his eyes as he looked down, "This was a mighty gladsome house once."

Cora had been a bright thing, pert as a bird on a bough. And like a bird, she would startle at a sound. He could build it all back now.

Cora in the room he had chosen for their hide-away. He reassuring her, when he left to scout the gorge outside. Her kiss at parting. "Hurry back, Ian. Hurry back to me." And then the loneliness of the caverns, the candle failing, flutter of a bat's wing or the crack of a bit of stone falling . . . and she had panicked. Most likely the candle went out too. In the dark she must have run out, calling him, turned toward the lake in her fright. The ledge, the drop into darkness . . . and womenfolk can't swim. Ink-horn Lake had taken her quickly, the soft suck of current drawing her down and under the ledge into

this grotto. And here her white bones had waited
. . . to be found by a child.

"Let's get back, young un," Ian heard himself say
at last. "If you want to venture around these caves,
I'll come with you. Won't take much work to widen
the notch. There's some mighty pretty things, stone-
built by the waters. Only I'll come with you, else you
mought git lost."

"Can Ma come?"

"If she ain't scairt."

"Ma's not scared of anything."

The judge, astride his big bay, rode on ahead.
Miles Winter carried the child on the pommel of his
saddle. And Esther Lorimer, on the delicate-hoofed
little mare, rode last, with the gaunt woodsman pacing beside her, his rifle in the crook of his arm.

Again Ian's mouth was dry. The voice of Esther
Lorimer was low-pitched. ". . . will have to return
East," she was saying. "If my husband had lived, we
might have made a home here. But the best land is
already taken up."

At the mouth of the gorge, Ian stopped and the
woman reined in. Beyond them lay the valley, crops
bright in fenced fields, cattle resting in the willow
shade. He lifted his eyes to the woman's face. Her
bonnet hung from one elbow, and the sun made her
tawny hair flash. The dark eyes rested on Ian, but her
gaze was not the provoking stare of tavern girls in

a town. Unsmiling, she stretched out her hand to him, and Ian barely touched it, trembling a little. The dark eyes held him.

Dry-mouthed, he said, "As for land, ma'am, there's a tolerable valley over west of here, 'bout a week's hard traveling. Grass stirrup high and a clear spring."

This time her smile struck through him like lightning through an oak. "It would be a noble thing to home in such a place, Mr. Farr. Won't you come along to the settlement with us, and tell us about your valley?"

As he strode on, Ian felt the lone comfort of the forest leaving him; the spell of witch water, drunk in sorrow long ago, was misting away. He surmised that she had let the judge and the merchant with little Martha ride on ahead. And then he knew, with a joy as bright as sunlight in a valley, that when the others passed out of sight around a bend in the road, she would rein in again and ask him to shorten her stirrup.

An Underground Episode
EDMUND WARE

Three figures leaned against the slanting rain—
Alamo Laska, Nick Christopher, and the boy who
had run away from home. They rested on their long-
handled shovels, and as they gazed into the crater,
which by their brawn they had hollowed in the earth,
the blue clay oozed back again, slowly devouring
the fruits of their toil.

Laska, the nomad, thought of the wild geese wing-
ing southward to warm bayous. Nick's heart, under
the bone and muscle of his great chest, swelled with
sweet thoughts of his wife and child, who lived in a
foreign city across an ocean. The boy felt the sting

of rain against his cheeks and dreamed of his mother, who seemed lovely and far away.

It was Sunday. The regular deep-trench gang lounged in their warm boardinghouse and drank dago red, while out on the job the three men toiled alone. They breathed heavily, and the gray steam crawled upon their backs, for it was cold.

"Look at 'er filling in," growled Laska. "Faster than a man could dig."

"Mud's get inna pipe," said Nick. "The inspector make us tear him out if she fill anymore."

Backed close to the edge of the crater stood a giant trench-digging machine. In the dusk it appeared as a crouched and shadowy animal—silent, gloomy, capable. But a broken piston had crippled its engines, and the men had swathed them in tarpaulin.

A long gray mound stretched away from the crater opposite the machine. Buried thirty feet below the mound was the new-laid sewer pipe. From the bottom of the pit at the machine, the pipe ran a hundred yards horizontally under the surface, opening in a manhole. This hundred yards of new-laid pipe was the reason for the three men digging in the rain. They had dug eleven hours, trying to uncover the open end of the pipe in order to seal it against the mud. But rain and ooze and storm had bested them. The bank had caved, and the mud had crawled into the mouth of the pipe, obstructing it.

"It's getting dark fast," said Laska, "an' we're licked."

"We can't do nothing more," said the boy.

Nick Christopher scraped the mud from his shovel. He looked up into the whirlpools of the sky. "In a year I go old country. I see my wife. I see my kid."

"Nick," said Laska, "go over to the shanty and get a couple of lanterns and telephone Stender. Tell him if he don't want the inspector on our tail to get out here quick with a gang."

Nick stuck his shovel in the mud and moved away across the plain toward the shanty.

The cold had crept into the boy. It frightened him, and in the darkness his eyes sought Laska's face. "How could we clean out the pipe, even when the gang got down to it?"

"Maybe we could flush it out with a fire hose," said Laska.

"There's no water plug within a mile."

Laska said nothing. The boy waited for him to reply, but he didn't. Picking up his damp shirt, the boy pulled it on over his head. He did not tuck in the tails, and they flapped in the wind, slapping against him. He looked like a gaunt, serious bird, striving to leave the ground. He was bareheaded, and his yellow hair was matted and stringy with dampness. His face was thin, a little sunken, and fine drops of moisture clung to the fuzz on his

79

cheeks. His lips were blue with cold. He was seventeen.

Laska stared into the pit. It was too dark to see bottom, but something in the black hole fascinated him. "If we could get a rope through the pipe, we could drag sandbags through into the manhole. That would clean her out in good shape."

"How could we get a rope through?"

"I dunno. Stender'll know." Laska walked over to the digging machine and leaned against its towering side. The rain had turned to sleet. "It's cold," he said.

The boy followed Laska and went close to him for warmth and friendship. "How *could* we get a rope through?"

Laska's shoulders lifted slowly. "You'll see. You'll see. You'll see when Stender gets here. Say, it's freezing."

After a long time of waiting, a yellow light flamed into being in the shanty, and they heard the muffled scraping of boots on the board floor. The shanty door opened. A rectangle of light stood out sharply.

Swart figures crossed and recrossed the lighted area, pouring out into the storm.

"Ho!" called Laska.

"Ho!" came the answer, galloping to them in the wind.

They heard the rasping of caked mud on dungarees, the clank of shovels, the voice of Stender, the foreman. Lanterns swung like yellow pendulums. Long-legged shadows reached and receded.

The diggers gathered about the rim of the pit, staring. Stender's face showed in the lantern light. His lips were wrinkled, as if constantly prepared for blasphemy. He was a tall, cursing conqueror. Orders shot from his throat, and noisily the men descended into the pit and began to dig. They drew huge, gasping breaths like mired beasts fighting for life.

The boy watched, his eyes bulging in the dark. Hitherto he had thought very briefly of sewers, regarding them as unlovely things. But Laska and Nick and Stender gave them splendor and importance. The deep-trench men were admirable monsters. They knew the clay, the feel and pattern of it, for it had long been heavy in their minds and muscles. They were big in three dimensions, and their eyes were black and barbarous. When they ate, it was with rough-and-tumble relish, and as their bellies fattened they spoke tolerantly of enemies. They played lustily with a view to satiation. They worked stupendously. They were diggers in clay, transformed by lantern light into a race of giants.

Through the rain came Stender, his black slicker crackling. "They're down," he said. "Angelo just struck the pipe."

Laska grunted.

Stender blew his nose with his fingers, walked away, and climbed down into the hole. They lost sight of him as he dropped over the rim. The sound of digging had ceased, and two or three men on the surface rested on their shovels, the light from below gleaming in their flat faces. Laska and the boy knew that Stender was examining the pipe. They heard him swearing at what he had found.

After a moment he clambered up over the rim and held up a lantern. His pipe, gripped firmly between his teeth, was upside down to keep out the wet. "Someone's got to go through the pipe," he said, raising his voice. "There's fifty bucks for the man that'll go through the pipe into the manhole with a line tied to his foot. Fifty bucks!"

There was a moment of quiet. The men thought of the fifty dollars and furtively measured themselves against the deed at hand. It seemed to the boy that he was the only one who feared the task. He did not think of the fifty dollars, but thought only of the fear. Three hundred feet through a rathole, eighteen inches in diameter. Three hundred feet of muck, of wet, black dark, and no turning back. But, if he did not volunteer, they would know that he was afraid. The boy stepped from behind Laska and said uncertainly, "I'll go, Stender," and he wished he might snatch back the words, for looking about him he saw that not a man among those present could have wedged his shoulders into the mouth of an eighteen-inch pipe. He was the only volunteer. They had known he would be the only one.

Stender came striding over, holding the lantern above his head. He peered into the boy's face. "Take off your clothes," he said.

"Take off my clothes?"

"That's what I said."

"You might get a buckle caught in a joint," said Laska. "See?"

The boy saw only that he had been trapped very cunningly. At home he could have been openly fearful, for at home everything about him was known. There, quite simply, he could have said, "I won't do it. I'm frightened. I'll be killed." But here the diggers in clay were lancing him with looks. And Laska was bringing a ball of line, one end of which would be fastened to his ankle.

"Just go in a sweater," said Laska. "A sweater an' boots over your woolens. We'll be waiting for you at the manhole."

He wanted so desperately to dive off into the night that he felt his legs bracing for a spring and a tight feeling in his throat. Then, mechanically, he began to take off his clothes. Nick had gone clumping off to the shanty, and shortly he returned with a pair of hip boots. "Here, kid. I get 'em warm for you inna shanty."

He thrust his feet into the boots, and Laska knelt and tied the heavy line to his ankle. "Too tight?"

"No. It's all right, I guess."

"Well—come on."

They walked past Stender, who was pacing up and down among the men. They slid down into the crater, deepened now by the diggers. They stood by the partly covered mouth of the pipe. They were thirty feet below the surface of the ground.

Laska reached down and tugged at the knot he had tied in the line; then he peered into the mouth of the tube. He peered cautiously, as if he thought it might be inhabited. The boy's glance wandered up the wet sides of the pit. Over the rim a circle of bland yellow faces peered at him. Sleet tinkled against lanterns, spattered down, and stung his flesh.

"Go ahead in," said Laska.

The boy blanched.

"Just keep thinking of the manhole, where you'll come out," said Laska.

The boy's throat constricted. He seemed to be bursting with a pressure from inside. He got down on his belly in the slushy ice and mud. It penetrated slowly to his skin and spread over him. He put his head inside the mouth of the pipe and drew back in horror. Some gibbering words flew from his lips. His voice sounded preposterously loud.

Laska's voice was already shopworn with distance. "You can make it! Go ahead."

He lay on his left side and, reaching out with his left arm, caught a joint and drew himself in. The mud oozed up around him, finding its way upon him, welling up against the left side of his face. He pressed his right cheek against the ceiling of the pipe to keep the muck from covering his mouth and nose. Laska's voice was far and muffled. Laska was in another world—a sane world of night, of storm, and the mellow glow of lanterns.

"Are you makin' it all right, kid?"

The boy cried out, his ears ringing with his cry. It reechoed from the sides of the pipe. The sides hemmed him, pinned him, closed him in on every side with their paralyzing circumference.

There is no darkness like the darkness underground that miners know. It borrows something from night, from tombs, from places used by bats. Such fluid black can terrify a flame, can suffocate and drench a mind with madness. There is a fierce desire to struggle, to beat one's hands against the prison. The boy longed to lift his pitiful human strength against the walls. He longed to claw at his eyes in the mad certainty that more than darkness curtained them.

He had moved but a few feet on his journey when panic swept him. Ahead of him the mud had built into a solid wave. Putting forth his left hand, he felt a scant two inches between the wave's crest and the ceiling of the pipe. There was nothing to do but go back. If he moved ahead, it meant death by suffocation. He tried to back away, but caught his toe in a joint of the pipe. He was entombed! In an hour he would be a body. The cold and dampness would kill him before they could dig down to him. Nick and Laska would pull him from the muck, and Laska would say, "Huh, his clock's stopped."

He thrashed with delirious strength against his prison. He felt the skin tearing from the backs of his hands as he flailed the rough walls. And some gods must have snickered, for above the walls of the pipe

85

were thirty feet of unyielding clay, eight thousand miles of earth below. A strength, a weight, a night, each a thousand times his most revolting dream, leaned upon the boy, depressing, crushing, stamping him out. The ground gave no cry of battle. It did no bleeding, suffered no pain, uttered no groans. It flattened him silently. It swallowed him in its foul despotism. It dropped its merciless weight upon his mind. It was so inhuman, so horribly incognizant of the God men swore had made it.

In the midst of his frenzy, when he had beaten his face against the walls until it bled, he heard a ringing voice he knew was real, springing from human sympathy. It was Laska, calling, "Are you all right, kid?"

In that instant the boy loved Laska as he loved his life. Laska's voice sheered the weight from him, scattered the darkness, brought him new balance and a hope to live.

"Fine!" he answered in a cracking yell. He yelled again, loving the sound of his voice and thinking how foolish yelling was in such a place.

With his left hand he groped ahead and found that the wave of mud had settled, leveled off by its own weight. He drew his body together, pressing it against the pipe. He straightened, moved ahead six inches. His fingers found a loop of oakum dangling from a joint, and he pulled himself on, his left arm forward, his right arm behind over his hip, like a swimmer's.

He had vanquished panic, and he looked ahead to victory. Each joint brought him twenty inches nearer his goal. Each twenty inches was a plateau, which enabled him to envision a new plateau—the next joint. The joints were like small, deceitful rests upon a march.

He had been more than an hour on the way. He did not know how far he had gone, a third, perhaps even a half of the distance. He forgot the present, forgot fear, wet, cold, blackness; he lost himself in dreaming of the world of men outside the prison. It was as if he were a small, superb island in hell.

He did not know how long he had been counting the joints, but he found himself whispering good numbers. "Fifty-one, fifty-two, fifty-three. . . ." Each joint, when he thought of it, appeared to take up a vast time of squirming in the muck, and the line dragged heavily behind his foot.

Suddenly, staring into the darkness so that it seemed to bring a pain to his eyes, he saw a pallid ray. He closed his eyes, opened them, and looked again. The ray was real, and he uttered a whimper of relief. He knew that the ray must come from Stender's lantern. He pictured Stender and a group of the diggers huddled in the manhole, waiting for him. The men and the manhole grew magnificent in his mind, and he thought of them worshipfully.

"Seventy-six, seventy-seven, seventy-eight. . . ."

The ray grew slowly, like a worthwhile thing. It took an oval shape, and the oval grew fat, like an egg, then round. It was a straight line to the manhole, and the mud had thinned.

Through the pipe into the boy's ears, a voice rumbled like halfhearted thunder. It was Stender's voice. "How you makin' it?"

"Oh, just fine!" His cry came pricking back into his ears like a shower of needles.

There followed a long span of numbness. The cold and wet had dulled his senses, so that whenever the rough ceiling of the pipe ripped his face, he did not feel it; so that struggling in the muck became an almost pleasant and normal thing, since all elements of fear and pain and imagination had been removed. Warmth and dryness became alien to him. He was a creature native to darkness, foreign to light.

The round yellow disk before him gave him his only sense of living. It was a sunlit landfall, luring him on. He would close his eyes and count five joints, then open them quickly, cheering himself at the perceptible stages of progress.

Then, abruptly it seemed, he was close to the manhole. He could hear men moving. He could see the outline of Stender's head as Stender peered into the mouth of the pipe. Men kneeled, pushing each other's head to one side, in order to watch him squirm toward them. They began to talk excitedly. He could hear them breathing, see details—and Stender and Laska reached in. They got their hands upon him. They hauled him to them, as if he were something they wanted to inspect scientifically. He felt as if they thought he was a rarity, a thing of great oddness. The light dazzled him. It began to move around and around and to dissolve into many lights, some of which danced locally on a bottle. He heard Stender's voice. "Well, he made it all right. What do you know?"

"Here, kid," said Laska, holding the bottle to his mouth. "Drink all of this that you can hold."

He could not stand up. He believed calmly that his flesh and bones were constructed of putty. He could hear no vestige of the song of victory he had dreamed of hearing. He looked stupidly at his hands, which bled painlessly. He could not feel his arms and legs at all. He was a vast sensation of lantern light and the steam of human beings breathing in a damp place.

Faces peered at him. The faces were curious and surprised. He felt a clouded, uncomprehending resentment against them. Stender held him up on one side, Laska on the other. They looked at each other across him. Suddenly Laska stooped and gathered him effortlessly into his arms.

"You'll get covered with mud," mumbled the boy.

"Damn if he didn't make it all right," said Stender. "Save us tearing out the pipe."

"Hell with the pipe," said Laska.

The boy's wet head fell against Laska's chest. He felt the rise and fall of Laska's muscles and knew that Laska was climbing with him up the iron steps inside the manhole. Night wind smote him. He

buried his head deeper against Laska. Laska's body
became a mountain of warmth. He felt a heavy, sigh-
ing peace, like a soldier who has been comfortably
wounded and knows that war for him is over.

The Cave

P. SCHUYLER MILLER

The cave measured less than a hundred feet from
end to end. It opened at the base of a limestone ridge
that rose like a giant, rounded fin out of the desert.
Its mouth was a flat oval, a shallow alcove scoured
out of the soft stone by wind and sand. Near one
end a smooth-walled tunnel sloped gently back into
the ridge. Twenty feet from the entrance it turned
sharply to the right and in a few feet swung back to
the left, paralleling its original course. Here it leveled
out into a broad, flat channel not more than four
feet high. This was the main chamber of the cave.

The big room, like the rest of the cave, had been
leached out of the limestone by running water, long

before. The water had followed a less resistant seam in the rock, dissolving out a passage whose low ceiling rose and fell a little with irregularities in the harder stratum overhead, whose floor was flat and water-polished in spots and in others, buried under a fine yellow clay. A little past the midpoint, the room opened out into a kind of inverted funnel in which a tall man could stand erect, a tapering chimney that quickly dwindled to a shaft barely big enough to admit a man's hand. Here the floor of the cave was lower, and the walls, which had drawn together until they were less than ten feet apart, were ribbed and terraced with flowstone.

Beyond the chimney the ceiling dropped suddenly to within a few inches of the floor. By lying flat on his face and squirming along between the uneven layers of rock, a thin man might have entered here. After measuring his length perhaps three times, he would have been able to raise himself on one elbow and twist into a sitting position, his back against the end wall of the cave and his head and shoulders wedged into a crevice that cut across the main passage at right angles. This crevice lay directly under the highest part of the ridge and vanished into darkness above and on either side. Water must at one time have flowed through it, for the harder siliceous layers in the limestone stood out on the walls in low relief like fine-ruled lines drawn in sooty black. Not even air stirred it now.

Twenty feet in the winding entry, six or eight feet

at the bend, another thirty to the chimney, and fifteen or twenty more to the back wall; it was a small cave.

The limestone of which the ridge was formed was perhaps the oldest exposed rock on the surface of that small, old world. It had been laid down in fairly deep water at a time when there were seas where there were only deserts now. There had been life in those seas; where wind or water had worn away the softer lime, their fossil bodies stood out from the surface of the gray stone. There were fluted shells like glistening black trumpets, swarms of tiny big-eyed things with fantastically shaped armor and many sprawling arms, long ropes of delicate, saw-edged weed whose fossil tissues were still stained a dull purple, occasionally fragments of some larger thing like an armored, blunt-headed fish. They had been alive, swarming and breeding in the shallow sea, when Earth was no more than a scabbed-over globe of slowly jelling flame.

The cave itself was very old. It had been made by running water, and it was a long time since there was much water on the dying world. Water, sour with soil acids leached from the black humus of a forest floor, had seeped down into the network of joint planes that intersected the flat-lying limestone beds, eating away the soft stone, widening cracks into crannies and crannies into high-arched rooms, rushing along the harder strata and tunneling through the softer ones, eventually bursting out into the open again at the base of a mossy ledge, and babbling away over the rocks to join a brook, a river, or the sea.

Millions of years had passed since there were rivers and seas on Mars.

Things change slowly underground. After a cave has died—after the sources of moisture that created it have shifted or dried up—it may lie without changing for centuries. A man may set his foot in the clay of its floor and go away, and another man may come a hundred or a thousand or ten thousand years afterward and see his footprint there, as fresh as though it had been made yesterday. A man may write on the ceiling with the smoke of a torch, and if there is still a little life in the cave and moisture in the rock, what he has written will gradually film over with clear stone and last forever. Rock may fall from the ceiling and bury portions of the floor or seal off some rooms completely. Water may return and wash away what has been written or coat it with slime. But if a cave has died—if water has ceased to flow and its walls and ceiling are dry—things seldom change.

Most of the planet's surface had been desert for more millions of years than anyone has yet estimated. From the mouth of the cave its dunes and stony ridges stretched away like crimson ripples left on a beach after a wave has passed. They were dust rather than sand: red, ferric dust ground ever finer by the action of grain against grain, milling over and over though the centuries. It lay in a deep drift in the alcove and spilled down into the opening of the cave; it carpeted the first twenty-foot passage as with a strip of red velvet, and a little of it passed around the angle in the tunnel into the short cross passage. Only the very finest powder, well-nigh impalpable, hung in the still air long enough to pass the second bend and reach the big room. Enough had passed to lay a thin, rusty mantle over every horizontal surface in the cave. Even in the black silt at the very back of the cave, where the air never stirred, there was a soft red bloom on the yellow flowstone.

The cave was old. Animals had sheltered in it. There were trails trodden into the dry clay, close to the walls, made before the clay had dried. There was no dust on these trails; animals still followed them when they needed to. There was a mass of draggled, shredded stalks and leaves from some desert plant, packed into the cranny behind a fallen rock and used as a nest. There were little piles of excreta, mostly the chitinous shells of insectlike creatures and the indigestible cellulose of certain plants. Under the chimney the ceiling was blackened by smoke, and there were shards of charcoal and burned bone mixed with the dust of the floor. There were places where the clay had been chipped and dug away to give more headroom or to make a flat place where a bowl could be set down. There were other signs as well.

* * *

The *grak* reached the cave a little after dawn. He had been running all night, and as the sun rose he had seen the shadow of the ridge drawn in a long black line across the crimson dunes and turned toward it. He ran with the tireless lope of the desert people, his splayed feet sinking only a little way into the soft dust where a man of his weight would have floundered ankle-deep.

He was a young male, taller than most of his kind, better muscled and fatter. His fur was sleek and thick, jet black with a pattern of rich brown. The colors in his cheek patches were fresh and bright, and his round black eyes shone like discs of polished coal.

He had been a hunter for less than one season. His tribe was one of the marauding bands that summered in the northern oases, raiding down into the lowlands in winter when the dry plateau became too cold and bare even for their hardy breed. It had fared better than most, for it had had little contact with man. The *grak* carried a knife, which he had made for himself out of an eight-inch bar of beryllium copper, taken in his first raid. It was the only human thing he owned. Its hilt was of bone, intricately carved with the clan symbols of his father line; its burnished blade was honed to a wicked double edge. It was the finest knife any of the desert folk had ever seen, and he had had to fight for it more than once. The desert tribes retained the old skills of metalworking, which the softer-living pastoral greenlanders had forgotten, and his tribe, the Begar, was among the best of the dryland smiths.

He wore the knife tucked into the short kilt of plaited leather that was his only garment. The old one of his father line had given it to him on the day he became a hunter and could no longer run naked like a cub. It was soft and pliable with long wear and oiled to a mahogany brown almost as dark and rich as his own chest patterns. There were black stains on it, which he knew were blood, for the old one had been one of the fiercest slayers of his line, and the kilt had come down to him from an even greater warrior in his own youth. The very pattern in which the thin strips of *zek* hide had been woven had lost its meaning, though it undoubtedly had been, and still was, of great virtue.

It was cold in the shadow of the ridge, and the *grak*'s long fur fluffed out automatically to provide extra insulation. He looked like a big black owl as he stood scanning the western sky, sniffing the wind with his beaklike nose. There was a tawny band low on the horizon, brightening as the sun rose. He had smelled a storm early in the night, for he had all the uncanny weather wiseness of his race and was sensitive to every subtle change in the quality of the atmosphere. He had started for the nearest arm of the greenlands, intending to claim the hospitality of the first village he could find, but the storm front was moving faster than he could run. He had seen the ridge only just in time.

He had recognized the place as he approached, though he had never seen it and none of his tribe had visited this part of the desert for many seasons. Such landmarks were part of the education of every dryland cub, and until they had become thoroughly ingrained in his wrinkled young brain he could not hope to pass the hunter's tests and win a hunter's rights. The cave was where he had known it would be, and he chuckled softly with satisfaction as he saw the weathered symbol carved in the stone over the opening. The desert people had long ago discarded the art of writing, having no use for it, but the meaning of certain signs had been passed down as a very practical part of their lore. This was a cave that the *grak*'s own forefathers had used and marked.

He studied the signs in the dust around the entrance of the cave. He was not the first to seek shelter there. The feathery membranes of his nose unfolded from their horny sheath, recording the faint scents that still hung in the thin air. They confirmed what his eyes had told him. The cave was occupied.

The wind was rising fast. Red dust devils whirled ahead of the advancing wall of cloud. Red plumes were streaming from the summit of every dune. Making the sign of peace, the *grak* stooped and entered the cave. Beyond the second bend in the passage was darkness, which not even his owl's eyes, accustomed to the desert nights, could penetrate. However, he did not need to see. The sensitive organs of touch that were buried in the gaudy skin of his cheek patches picked up infinitesimal vibrations in the still air and told him accurately where there were obstacles. His ears were pricked for the slightest sound. His nose picked up a mixture of odors—his own characteristic scent, the dry and slightly musty smell of the cave itself, and the scents of the other creatures with which he would have to share it.

He identified them, one by one. There were four or five small desert creatures, which had more to fear from him than he from them. There was one reptilian thing, which under other circumstances might be dangerous, and which still might be if the peace were broken. And there was a *zek*.

The carnivore was as big and nearly as intelligent as the tribesman himself. Its kind waged perpetual war on the flocks of the greenland people and rarely visited the oases, but when one did wander into the desert it was the most dreaded enemy of the dryland tribes. It stole their cubs from beside their very campfires and attacked full-grown hunters with impunity. Its mottled pelt was the choicest prize a hunter could bring back as proof of his prowess. To some of the more barbaric tribes of the north it was more than just a beast—it was His emissary.

A sudden gust from the passage at his back told the *grak* that the storm was breaking. In a matter of minutes the air would be unbreathable outside. Softly, so as not to arouse the savage beast's suspicions, he began to murmur the ritual of the peace. His fingers were on the hilt of his knife as he began, but as the purring syllables went out into the hollow darkness, his nostrils told him that the fear odor was diminishing. Somewhere in the dark a horny paw scuffed on the dry clay, and there was an instant reek of terror from some of the smaller things, but the *zek* made no sign. It was satisfied to keep the peace.

Moving cautiously, the *grak* found a hollow in the wall near the entry and sat down to wait, squatting with his knees tucked up close under his furry belly, the hard rock at his back. The knife he laid on the floor beside his hand, where it would be ready if he needed it. For a time his senses remained keyed to fever pitch, but gradually his tenseness eased. They were all *grekka* here—all living things, united in the common battle for existence against a cruel and malignant Nature. They knew the law and the brotherhood, and they would keep the truce as long as the storm lasted. Gradually the nictitating lids slipped across his open eyes, and he sank into a half sleep.

Harrigan blundered into the cave by pure luck. He knew nothing about Mars or its deserts except what the Company put in its handbook, and that was damn little. He was a big man and a strong man, born in the mountains with a more-than-ordinary tolerance for altitude, and he had had to spend less than a week in the dome before they shifted him to the new post in the eastern Sabaeus. He did what he was told and no more than he was told, laid away his pay every week in anticipation of one almighty spree when they brought him in at the next opposition, and had nothing but contempt for the native Martians. *Grekka* they were called, and that was all he knew or cared about them. To him they looked like animals and they were animals, in spite of the fact that they could talk and build houses and kept herds of peg-legged monstrosities that seemed to serve as cattle. Hell—parrots could talk and ants kept cattle!

Harrigan had been a miner on Earth. He was that here, but he couldn't get used to the idea that plants could be more valuable than all the copper and tungsten and carnotite in the world. The desert and its barren red hills nagged at him, and whenever he could get time off he explored them. The fact that he found only rocks and sand did nothing to extinguish his sullen conviction that there was treasure incalculable here somewhere if only the damned natives would talk or the Company would listen to a man who knew minerals better than the big shots knew the swing of their secretaries' hips.

The fact was, of course, as the Company knew very well, that Martian mineral deposits had been exhausted by a native Martian civilization pursuing its inevitable way to an inevitable end at a time when Adam and Eve probably had tails. That the descendants of that civilization were still alive, even on a basis of complete savagery, spoke volumes for the stamina of the native race. Such arguments, however, would have meant less than nothing to a man of Harrigan's type. There were mines on Earth. There were mines on the moon. Hell—there were mines on Mars!

This time he had overstayed his luck. To him the low yellow wall of cloud on the western horizon was only a distant range of hills, which he might someday visit and where he might find wealth enough to set him up in liquor for the rest of his life. He had spent the night in the cab of his sand car, and it was not until the clouds were a sullen precipice towering halfway up the sky that he understood what he was heading into. He swung around and headed back, but by then it was too late.

When the storm hit it was like night. The air was a semisolid mass through which the sand car wallowed blindly with only its instrument board to show where it was going. Dust swiftly clogged the air intake, and he had to take out the filters, put on his mask, and hope for the best. It didn't come. In seconds the air inside the cab was a reddish mist, and dust was settling like fine red pepper on every exposed surface. The wind seized the squat machine and rocked it like a skiff in a typhoon, but Harrigan could only hang on, peer red-eyed through dust-coated goggles at his dust-covered instruments, and wonder where he was.

The floundering car climbed painfully to the top of a monster dune, pushed its blunt snout out over the steep leading edge, slewed violently around, and started down. Harrigan yanked despairingly at the steering levers; they were packed tight with dust and refused to move. He did not see the ridge until the car smashed head-on into it. There was a despairing gurgle from the engine, a last clatter of broken bearings, and the car stopped. At once sand began to pile up behind and around it, and Harrigan, picking himself up off the floor of the cab, saw that if he didn't get out fast he would be buried where he sat.

He struggled out on the lee side of the car into a gale that bit into him like an icy knife. He could not see the car when he had taken one step away from it. The dust drove through every seam and patch of his clothes and filtered in around the edges of his mask. It was sucked into his mouth and nose and gritted under his swollen eyelids. It was everywhere, and in no time it would smother him.

The car was lost, though he was probably less than ten feet from it. The wind screamed past him in unholy glee, tearing at every loose flap on his coat, chilling him to the bone. He took half a dozen blundering steps, knee-deep in the soft dust, stumbled, and came down on his knees at the foot of the cliff. His outthrust hands met solid rock. He struggled forward on his knees and peered at it through crusted goggles. It was limestone, and where there was limestone there might be a cave. Foot by foot he felt his way along the uneven surface of the ridge until suddenly it dropped away in front of him. He staggered forward and fell on his hands and knees in the entrance of a cave.

His head had clipped the low overhang as he fell, and it was a minute or two before he realized where he was. Almost automatically then he crawled ahead until his skull rammed hard into another wall. He sat gingerly back on his heels and clawed at his mask. It was completely plugged with dust and utterly useless. He lifted it off his face and took a slow breath. There was dust in the air—and plenty of it—but he could breathe.

He groped about him in the pitch dark, found an opening in the right-hand wall, and crawled in. Almost immediately there was another sharp turn, and the passage suddenly opened out on either side and left him crouching at the entrance of what he knew must be a good-sized room.

Harrigan knew caves too well to take chances with them. What lay ahead might be a room or it might be a pit dropping to some lower level. He had a feeling that it was big. He found the corner where the left-hand wall swung back, moved up against it, moistened his lips with a thick, dry tongue, and shouted, "Hoy!"

The echo rattled back at him like gunfire. The place was big but not too big. What he needed now was water and a light.

He had both. Dust had worked in around the stopper of his canteen until he could barely start the threads, but one last savage twist of his powerful fingers did the trick. There wasn't much left. He let a few drops trickle over his tongue and down his throat, wiped the caked dust off the threads with a finger, and screwed the cap back on. These storms lasted for days sometimes, and it was all the water in the world as far as he was concerned.

Light came next. Harrigan had spent too much time underground to be afraid of the dark, but it was plain common sense to want to see what you were getting into. Harrigan hated mysteries. If he knew what he was facing he could fight his way through anything, but he hated blind fumbling and he hated the dark.

Enough water had evaporated from the open canteen in the minute or two he had had the cap off to raise appreciably the moisture content of the cave— at least for the Martians. To their acute senses it was the equivalent of a heavy fog.

A few feet away in the blackness the *grak* awoke with a start. Farther back in the cave one of the small animals stirred eagerly. And the *zek* sneezed.

Harrigan's blundering approach had roused the occupants of the cave, and every eye, ear, and nose had been trained on him when he appeared. One rodentlike creature made a panicky rush as it got his scent, only to freeze in terror as it nearly bumped into the *zek*. The peace, for the moment, was suspended. A new factor had entered the situation, and a new equilibrium must be reached. They quietly awaited developments.

Harrigan had missed all this preliminary activity in his efforts to find out where he was, rub the dust out of his eyes, and get a few drops of water down his parched gullet. But when the *zek* sneezed, the sudden sound was like an explosion in his ears. In the dead silence that followed, he could clearly hear the sound of quiet breathing. It was close to him, and it came from more than one place. He had to have a light!

There should have been a torch in the pocket of his coverall. There wasn't. He had lost it or left it in the car. He had a lighter, though. He ripped feverishly at the zipper of his coverall. It slid open a few inches with a sound like the crackle of lightning and jammed. Sweat dripping from his forehead, he sat back on his heels and fumbled for his gun, but there was no movement from the things in the dark. Slowly and softly he slipped two fingers into his pocket and found the lighter. Leveling the gun at the blank blackness in front of him, he lifted the lighter above his head and flipped off the cap.

The burst of yellow flame was dazzling. Then he saw their eyes—dozens of little sparks of green and red fire staring out of the dark. As his own eyes adjusted he saw the *grak,* huddled like a woolly black gargoyle in his corner. The Martian's huge, round

106

eyes were watching him blankly, his grinning mouth was slightly open over a saw-edged line of teeth, and his pointed ears were spread wide to catch every sound. His beaklike, shining nose and bright-red cheek patches gave him the look of a partly plucked owl. He had a wicked-looking knife in his spidery fingers.

Harrigan's gaze flickered around the circle of watching beasts. He knew nothing of Martian animals, except for a few domesticated creatures the greenlanders kept, and they made a weird assortment. They were mostly small, ratty things with big eyes and feathery antennae in place of noses. Some of them were variously decorated with fantastic collections of colored splotches, crinkled horns, and faceted spines, which presumably were attractive to themselves or their mates. At the far end of the cave, curled up in a bed of dry grass, was a lean, splotched thing, almost as big as the little native, which stared at him with malevolent red eyes set close together over a grinning, crocodilian snout. As he eyed it, it yawned hideously and dropped its head on its crossed forepaws—paws like naked, taloned hands. It narrowed its eyes to crimson slits and studied him insolently from under the pallid lids. It looked nasty, and his fingers closed purposefully over the butt of his gun.

The *grak*'s cackle of protest stopped him. The only word he could make out was *bella*—peace. He knew that because he had had a woman named Bella

back in New York, or he had had before he signed
on with the Company. Besides, it was part of the
spiel you were supposed to rattle off every time you
talked to one of the damned little rats. It was all the
Martian he knew, so he spat it out, keeping one eye
on the other beast.

This was the first man the *grak* had ever seen. It
was a monstrous-looking thing, wrapped in layer
after layer of finely plaited fabric, which must have
taken his mates many years to weave, even if their
clumsy fingers were as deft as those of the greenlanders, who occasionally did such things. A thrilling
philosophical problem was teasing the *grak*'s young
brain. Was or was not this man of the *grekka*?

To a native Martian the term *grekka* means lit-
erally "living things." Any creature native to the
planet is a *grak*; all of them, separately or collec-
tively, are *grekka*. The first men to come in contact
with the native race heard the word used to desig-
nate the Martians themselves and assumed that it
was the Martian equivalent of "men." Graziani, of
course, as an anthropologist of note, immediately
realized the truth of the matter—the situation is
duplicated again and again among human aborigines
—but the label stuck. Nor did that matter too much,
for *grekka* did include the natives and made perfectly good sense when it was used as men proceeded
to use it. What did matter was that the word was

also the key to the whole elaborate structure of Martian psychology.

Millions of years of unceasing struggle with the forces of an inclement environment on a swiftly maturing and rapidly dying planet have ingrained in the native Martian race, greenlanders and drylanders alike, the fundamental concept that Nature is their undying enemy. Life for them is a bitter fight again overwhelming odds with an invisible foe who will use every possible means to grind out the little spark of ego in each round, furry Martian skull. You find it in the oldest legends: always the wily native hero is outwitting—there is no other word for it—the evil purposes of the personified, malignant universe.

Grekka is the ultimate expression of this grim philosophy. In the battle for life, all living things —all *grekka*—are brothers. No Martian would ever dispute the theory of evolution; it is the very core of his existence that all beasts are brothers. That is a somewhat oversimplified statement of the fact, for from there on *grekka* becomes entangled in the most elaborate maze of qualifications and exceptions that a once highly civilized race has been able to devise over a period of millions of years. Your native Martian, drylander or greenlander, will help his brother beast whenever the latter is clearly losing out in a battle with Nature, but there are certain things that the individual is supposed to be able to do for himself if he is not to give unholy satisfaction to Him—the Great Evil One—the personification of the universal doom that pours unending misfortune on all *grekka* alike.

The distinction is one of those things that no logician will ever be able to work out. It is one thing for the desert tribes and something else for the low-landers. The Begar will draw the line at something that is a sacred duty of every Gorub, in spite of the fact that the two tribes have lived side by side on a more or less friendly basis for generations. One clan —even one father line—may and must act in ways that no other clan on Mars may duplicate without eternally losing a varying number of points in its game with Him and His aides.

What puzzled the young *grak* of the cave was whether man—specifically Harrigan—was *grekka*. If he was, he was an innate member of the brotherhood of living things and subject to its laws. If he wasn't, then he could only be a personification or extension of the inimical First Principle Himself and, hence, an inherent enemy. Since the time of Graziani and the Flemming expedition, every Martian native, individual by individual and tribe by tribe, has had to make this decision for himself, and by it govern his further relations with humanity. The Begar had had too little contact with mankind to have needed to make such a decision as a tribe. Now the young *grak* decided to reserve judgment, keep his eyes open, and let the man prove himself by his further actions.

Harrigan, of course, knew absolutely nothing of all this. It would probably not have mattered if he had. What some damned animal thought about the universe was nothing to him.

For a moment there had been death in the air. Now the tension was vanishing. The smaller animals were settling down again, the little *grak* grinning and nodding as he squatted down in the corner. Only the *zek*'s slitted eyes were still studying him with cold indifference. The damned nightmare was curled up in the one place in the cave where a man could stand up! Harrigan gave it eye for eye, and all the little furry and scaly creatures lifted their heads and watched them while the *grak* blinked worriedly. They could all smell the hostility between the two. The *zek* yawned again, showing an evil double line of knife-edged fangs and a leprous white gullet, and flexed the mighty muscles that lay like slabs of molded steel across its massive shoulders. Harrigan sat glumly down where he was, his back against the cold stone, his gun on the floor beside him, the lighter wedged into a crack in the rock between his feet.

Outside the storm was at its height. The far-off screaming of the wind echoed and reechoed in the big room. Puffs of red dust drifted in out of the

111

darkness, and the flame of the lighter wavered and danced. In the occasional lulls, the only sound in the cave was their steady breathing. Every eye, Harrigan knew, was on him. He was the intruder here, and they were wary of him. Let 'em be! A man was something to *be* afraid of on this damned little dried-up world!

He glowered back at them, making up malicious fantasies about their probable habits. There were plenty of fancy stories going the rounds about how these Martians went at things. He grinned sardonically at the little *grak* as he recalled one particularly outrageous libel.

The *grak* smiled reassuringly back at him. This man was a hideous travesty of a thing, but he was keeping the peace.

Harrigan sized up the cave. It wasn't a bad hole as caves went. It was dry, the angle in the passage kept the dust out, and it was big enough so a man could stretch. With a fire and water he could last as long as the storm would.

There had been a fire, he noticed, under the chimney at the far end of the cave. There was soot on the ceiling, and the rock had the crumbled look of burned limestone. It was too close to the big beast for comfort, though. That was a wicked-looking brute if ever there was one. Better leave him be, but if he tried to start anything, James Aloysius Harrigan would show him who was tough!

A gust stronger than any that had come before

bent the thin flame of the lighter far over, drawing it out into a feeble yellow thread. Harrigan bent quickly and sheltered it with his cupped palms. It seemed smaller and duller than when he had first lit it. He picked up the lighter and shook it close to his ear. It was almost dry! He snapped down the cap.

The darkness that fell was stifling. The invisible walls of the cave seemed to be closing in on him, compressing the thin air, making it hard to breathe. The dust got into his nose and throat. It had a dry, metallic taste. Iron in it. It shriveled the membranes of his throat like alum. He cleared his throat noisily and ran his tongue over his thick lips. What he needed was a drink. Just a couple of drops. He unscrewed the canteen and lifted it to his lips.

Somewhere in the blackness something moved. It made only the very smallest sound—the tick of a claw on the rock—but he heard it. Instantly he was on the alert. So that was their game! Well, let 'em come! They were as blind as he was in this hole, and he had yet to see the day when any animal could outsmart him!

He set the canteen carefully down behind a block of stone. It would be safer there if there was a scrap, and it might hit against something and give him away if he carried it. Shifting his gun to his left hand, he began cautiously to work his way along the wall, stopping every few inches to listen. He could hear nothing but the rhythmic, ghostly whisper of the creatures' breathing. Whatever it was that had moved, it was quiet now.

His fingers found the first of the slabs of fallen limestone, which lay half buried in the clay along the right-hand wall. They reached almost to the chimney, but about fifteen feet from where he had been sitting there was a break in the line, and the wall dropped back into a shallow alcove no more than two feet high. In there he would have solid rock on all sides of him, and he would be directly opposite the pile of dried weeds in which the *zek* was lying. He would have a clear shot at the ugly brute between two of the fallen blocks.

His groping hand came down on something cold and scaly that wriggled hastily away under the rocks. There was an answering squeal of terror and a patter of scampering feet as panic-stricken little creatures scattered in front of him. Something as heavy as a cat landed on his back and clung there, chattering madly. He batted at it and knocked it to the floor. Then, only a few feet ahead in the darkness, he heard the stealthy click of claw on stone again. The *zek*!

He had to have light! It was suicide to face that monster in pitch blackness! He had slipped the lighter back into the outside pocket of his coverall. He fumbled for it. It was gone!

The panic went out of Harrigan in a flash. He sat back on his heels and curled his fingers lovingly around the butt of his gun. The tougher things got, the better he liked them. The lighter must have dropped out of his open pocket; he could find it when he needed it by going back over the ground he had just covered. It wasn't lost. But he didn't need it. The dark was his protection, not his enemy. They couldn't see him in the dark.

He dropped back on all fours. Everything was quiet again. He'd hear them if they tried anything. He was almost at the alcove, and then they'd have to blast to get at him. He could pick 'em off one by one if they tried to get in.

The clay was hard as brick and full of little chunks of broken stone that gouged at his knees, even through the heavy suit. The roof was lower, too; he had to get down on his elbows and hitch along, almost flat on his face.

His heart was thumping like mad. He was working too hard in this thin air. He rolled over on his side, his back against one of the big blocks, and stared into the blackness. Another few feet and he could lie down and wait for them. He needed time out. He had to have a clear head. He cursed his stupidity in not bringing an oxygen flask from the car. One shot of that stuff and he'd be ready to take 'em on all at once, barehanded!

As he started on again something tinkled on the stone beside him. He groped for it; it was the lighter. It had been in his back pocket. Damn fool—letting the darkness rattle him! Animals were all afraid of fire. He could smoke 'em out any time he wanted to. He was boss of this cave! A grin of satisfaction spread over his grimy face as he shuffled along on knees and elbows through the dust.

One big slab almost blocked the hole he was looking for. It was a tight squeeze, but he wriggled through and found plenty of room behind it. He felt for the crack between the blocks that was opposite the nest, slid his gun cautiously into position, and flashed the lighter. Now!

The nest was empty.

With a curse Harrigan rolled to the other opening. The flame of the lighter showed him the far end of the cave—the *grak* crouching wide-eyed in his niche, the black arch of the entrance, and the *zek*!

The thing had slipped past him in the dark. It stood where he had been sitting a moment ago, by the entrance. It stared back at him over its shoulder, a hideous thing like a giant reptile-snouted weasel, mottled with leprous gray. It grinned at him, its red eyes mocking, then stretched out a handlike paw and picked up his canteen!

Harrigan's first shots spattered against the rock above the monster's head; the light blinded him. His next clipped through the coarse mane on the back of its thick neck. His last was fired point-blank into its snarling face. Then the lighter went spinning away across the floor, and talons like steel clamps closed on his arm.

The rocks saved him. The thing had him by the arm, but his body was protected. He still had the gun; he twisted around in the beast's grim grasp and emptied it into the darkness. Its grip loosened, and he snatched his arm free. It was bleeding where the *zek*'s claws had bitten into the flesh. Then, through the crack on his right, he saw a sheet of white flame go up as the lighter touched the powder-dry mass of weeds in the beast's nest.

The cave was lit up as bright as day. Harrigan saw the *zek,* blood streaming from a ragged wound in its broad chest, its face a bloody mask of fury. One shot had plowed a long furrow across the side of his head. It gathered its powerful hind legs under it, seized a corner of the great block that barred the opening with paws like human hands, and pulled. The muscles stood out in knotted ropes on its arms and shoulders as it worried at the massive stone. Then the packed clay at its base crumbled, and the great block slowly tipped. The way was open. His sanctuary had become a trap.

There was one way out. Harrigan took it. Desperately he lunged forward, out of the cranny straight into the thing's arms. He clamped both hands over its narrow lower jaw and forced its slavering snout straight back with all the power of his own broad back. It rose on its haunches, hugging him to it, then toppled over, dragging him with it into the open, raking him with its cruel hind claws. He set his jaws and felt his arms stiffen and straighten as the evil head was driven back—back. As through a red mist he saw the *grak*'s owl eyes staring at him over the monster's shoulder, saw the coppery gleam of firelight on a shining knife. He felt the *zek* shudder as the keen blade was driven home in its back. It began to cough, great racking coughs that shook its whole frame. Its arms tightened convulsively about him, and its claws clenched in his back as the copper knife drove home again and again. Then, slowly, they began to loosen. The beast was dead.

The burning weeds had dimmed to a dull flicker. The dust that had been stirred up in their struggle hung like a red veil in the air. Harrigan lay staring up through it at the little native, sucking the thin air painfully into his tortured lungs. The damned little rat had saved his life! He wiped the blood and dust off his face with his sleeve and got slowly to his feet. He had to stoop to clear the ceiling. That knife— that was a man's weapon. Wonder where the *grak* got it—

He took one step toward the *grak*. Before he could take another the knife went smoothly into his belly, just under the breastbone, driving upward to the heart.

Squatting in the darkness, listening to the distant murmur of the storm, the *grak* wondered what would have happened in the cave if the man had not come there. The *zek* had been a treacherous ally; sooner or later it might have broken the peace. Once its blood rage had been aroused it had, of course, been necessary to kill it. But if the man had not come that necessity might have been averted.

The man had been very clever. The *grak* had been almost certain that he was what he pretended to be. But as always there was one thing—one very little thing—to betray him. He did not know the law of water.

In every doubtful situation, the *grak* reflected smugly, there was some trivial matter in which the Source of Evil or His emissaries would reveal themselves. Some one thing in which the true *grak* was clearly distinguishable from the forces of Nature against which he must forever fight. One must be quick to see such discrepancies—and quick to act on them.

The matter of water lay at the very root of the law by which all *grekka*—living things—existed. It was the thing that all must have, which none, under the law, could withhold from another. Without it there could be no life. With it every living thing was given strength to battle on against the eternal foe.

The man had brought water to the cave. Under the law, all *grekka* must share in it according to their need. But when the *zek* had gone to take its share, the man had tried to kill it. By that small thing he revealed himself—no *grak,* but one of His evil things. So he had died. So once more was victory won for the brotherhood of living things against the universe.

He would make a song about this thing and sing it by the fires of his tribe. He would cut a sign in the stone over the entrance of the cave after the storm was over, so that others who came there would know of it. And the cave itself, where his forefathers had come and lit their fires, would keep the bodies of the *zek* and the man thus, side by side, as witness forever.

Lindbergh
and the Underground Lake

ROBERT F. BURGESS

Every major achievement usually triggers a steady
progression of firsts. The first man to jump off a cliff,
flapping his arms to fly like a bird, inspired another
to be first to try it a different way. The Wright brothers' first successful flight at Kitty Hawk in 1903 led
to Charles Lindbergh's first successful transatlantic
flight in 1927. Similarly Cousteau's invention of the
aqualung, which freed man for unrestrained underwater flights, provided the means for that transat-
lantic-aviator's son, Jon Lindbergh, to make the first
successful United States cave dive.

121

In March, 1953, the twenty-year-old marine-biology student from Stanford University volunteered to swim alone into California's Bower Cave. It was no publicity stunt, no act of bravado. It was simply something he wanted to do quietly on his own. Lindbergh's curiosity had been whetted by a theory that the clear, cool popular swimming spa in the gold-bearing hills of northern California was fed from a secret inner chamber. When the man behind the theory, San Francisco speleologist Raymond de Saussure, organized an expedition to learn its whereabouts, Lindbergh offered to make the exploratory dives.

Their first visit was to reconnoiter the pool. Since no one else was a diver, all efforts were directed toward assisting Lindbergh. The water in the pool was cold, clear, and deep. Besides a single-tank aqualung, dive mask, and flippers, he wore a hooded rubber dry suit to keep himself warm. A six-inch Army trench knife was strapped to his leg. He carried a waterproof flashlight, a carbon-dioxide-inflatable, rubber diver's float to buoy him if necessary, and two small tanks of oxygen in case of an emergency. For safety's sake, his companions tied a light nylon line around his waist.

A crowd of curious spectators watched the burdened diver swim out into the pool and sink from sight. Some wondered about the young man's sanity, but then they came by this naturally. Their fathers once wondered the same thing about a young man determined to try and fly single-handed across the Atlantic Ocean.

Less awkward now that he was submerged with all of his gear, Lindbergh cruised along just below the surface, examining the basin. As he descended for a closer look, the chill of the water penetrated his thin rubber suit. Increased water pressure molded it tightly to his body in folds and creases that would leave their red welts on his skin long after the dive.

Carefully he scrutinized the fretted niches and fractured limestone walls, stretching into the dim green depths below him. The unfamiliar line tugged at his waist. He pulled more slack, then dropped deeper. Pain built in his ears. He worked his jaws, and the pressure equalized with a begrudging squeak that instantly eased the discomfort.

The underwater basin grew larger as the walls receded; cautiously he moved into the shadow of an overhang. Below him, he saw what it concealed—the huge black opening of a cave. It was about thirty feet high. Long, jagged, toothlike rocks thrust down into the awesome maw.

Lindbergh paused before it, gathering slack in his safety line and probing the cavern's inner darkness with the thin yellow beam of his flashlight. Despite the general loss of daylight under the limestone overhang, the water visibility was still good. He could see with his flashlight for twenty-five to fifty feet.

123

Staying well below the overhead rock snags, he moved into the cave, playing the beam of light back and forth in front of him. Slowly he swam about 150 feet along the gradually rising tunnel, his rhythmic exhalations rumbling loud in his ears. Suddenly he saw his air bubbles cease forming the flattened silvery balloons that marked his progress along the roof of the passageway. Instead, they disappeared overhead and were replaced by ripples. The bubbles were breaking on a surface; an air pocket was above him.

Lindbergh rose cautiously, an arm overhead in case it was only a shallow cavity in the ceiling. He did not want to shoot up headfirst into a thin air pocket only inches away from skull-fracturing rock.

His hand went through the invisible barrier first, then the rest of him, his heart pounding as he surfaced with a loud slapping and echoing of waves in a large air pocket. Saussure was right! It was the chamber they were looking for!

Lindbergh pushed up his mask and looked around. It was a large, vaulted room. Long, slender stalactites reached down from the ceiling, glittering wetly in the beam of his light. In some places along the undulating limestone walls he saw brilliant white cascades that looked like stiffly starched curtains. He snapped off his flashlight. The room was immediately plunged into darkness. But as his eyes slowly adjusted, he began to see the vague outlines of the

124

walls reflected in a dim light from the underwater entrance.

After a last look at the room, Lindbergh retraced his way down through the siphon, coiling his line as he went. He was anxious to tell the others what he had found.

Lindbergh and his friends returned to the resort the following month. During the intervening weeks he had figured out a way to photograph the inside of the cave and show them what he had seen.

Today this might seem like a trivial chore, but in the early 1950's it was a bit more complicated. Waterproof cameras were not readily available then. If a diver was to photograph underwater, he usually built his own waterproof, wooden box with a glass port or fashioned something more costly and elaborate of metal. Since no such equipment was available to Lindbergh, he planned to use an ordinary small camera, flashbulbs, and reflector that he could wrap in plastic bags until he got them inside the underground room to take his pictures.

This time he would make two journeys into the cave—the first to take in a collapsed rubber raft to inflate and use as a dry, stable platform from which to photograph, and the second trip with his camera.

Getting the one-man raft from the pool to the underground lake was slightly awkward. Despite its small size, the thing was determined to float prematurely. During Lindbergh's long swim through the siphon, he kept the ungainly bundle clutched to his chest with all the determination of a quarterback driving for a badly needed first down.

Once again surfacing inside the chamber, he unfolded the raft and ducked underwater to inflate it. As he tried to manipulate the raft, his flashlight, and the cylinder of compressed carbon dioxide all at the same time, he wished for at least two more hands. Somehow, however, he got the gas cylinder attached and turned on.

With a *whoosh* the raft inflated and popped to the surface. There it continued to balloon into a grotesque rubber bubble, while Lindbergh fumbled frantically to shut off the oversized cylinder of gas that he now realized was too big for the job. Seconds before the weirdly swollen craft would have burst its seams, he stemmed the flow.

Bobbing around on the surface, he hastily valved off excess gas until the raft shrank back to normal and floated more supinely. Lindbergh quickly checked its seams for bubbles. It was all right. The stage was set. He clamped his jaws on his mouthpiece and swam back down the siphon to the other pool.

The next morning Lindbergh checked all his gear for the last time. Camera, flash, and bulbs seemed waterproof enough in their triple thickness of plastic bags. If anything leaked, the entire two-day dive would be wasted. So he made doubly sure that the package was well sealed and tied to his flashlight before he entered the pool and dived.

Again Lindbergh made his way into the siphon. As he passed its entrance, his lifeline snagged on the jagged rocks. Caught in midstroke, he went back and freed the line without difficulty. How deep was this hidden lake? he wondered. Aiming his light down, he began a vertical descent, finning slowly toward an unseen bottom. The yellow beam of his flashlight pierced the green darkness like a slender probing finger, reaching for something it could not touch. It never crossed Lindbergh's mind that if his only light went out he would be left suspended in an inky void, blindly trying to find his way back to the surface without crashing into some obstacle.

When nothing solid appeared in his moving beam, he more carefully noted his progress on the slowly moving black hand of his depth gauge. With some surprise that he had not found bottom yet, he continued down—70 . . . 90 . . . 100 feet. Finally, at 120 feet, he stopped and swept his light below him in wide arcs. Water clarity was perfect, but there was still no bottom. By then he was apparently beginning to feel the first effects of nitrogen narcosis, because, as he later reported, "I found I had difficulty concentrating on more than one thing. I looked at the depth gauge and would forget about the rope. I would remember the rope with something of a shock. As soon as I went to a depth of 60 feet, there was no trouble at all."

Lindbergh returned to the surface of the hidden lake. With a sweep of his light, he picked out the pale oval shape of his raft. He swam to it, dropped his light and camera package inside, and prepared to climb in. He got one leg over the side, but in the process he flooded the raft.

He tried scooping out the water, but was hindered by his heavy diving gear. Finally he towed the water-logged raft over to the side of the chamber, tied it to a stalactite, and began shucking his cumbersome equipment. He put his weight belt in the bottom of the raft and tied his aqualung beside it. Lacking an implement to bail out the raft, he used his face mask. The raft was almost empty when he accidentally hit his air tank and smashed the glass in his mask.

Muttering darkly to himself, Lindbergh climbed into the raft to ponder the situation. The loss of the mask meant that he would be virtually blind trying to find his way out of the cave. But he thought he would at least be able to see well enough to follow the reflected daylight through the siphon back into the pool. About then he realized he had also torn a fist-sized hole in the seat of his rubber suit. It provided him with a chilly reminder that if a piece of his broken face-mask glass sliced a similar hole in the raft, his tank, weights, and all could sink from under him. Then there would be no way out of the cave.

Lindbergh cautiously felt around the bottom of the rubber raft and threw stray pieces of broken glass overboard. Next he placed the camera package in his lap and unwrapped it. He attached the flash, set the shutter speed at 1/25 of a second, and methodically shot a roll of pictures of the cave's interior. Then he repacked and sealed the equipment for his return trip through the siphon.

Donning his diving gear again, Lindbergh held his nose and dived down toward the blurred semicircle of light marking the mouth of the siphon. Once he negotiated the sharp rock pendants at the entrance, he had no trouble swimming up into the basin where his waiting friends gave him a hero's welcome.

The incident of the torn suit and smashed mask in no way dampened Lindbergh's desire to explore this new-found system more thoroughly. In fact, he stayed out of the water only long enough to get another face mask and stick a tire patch on his seat, and then he dived back through the siphon. This time he swam 300 feet back into the cave, at which point he felt dizzy and returned to the basin. The last he saw of his one-man raft, it was still drifting aimlessly around the hidden underground lake, deep within Bower Cave.

The Bottomless Well
WALTER S. TERRY

Single file they walked down the rocky trail that he had not traveled in thirty years—not since he was Carol's age. Carol followed a few steps behind him, and Mike, Carol's shadow, placed his tennis-shoed feet deliberately where hers had been.

"How much farther is it, Daddy?" Carol said in the measured tones of her solemn adolescence.

David looked around at her, seeing the brisk movement of her bare legs under a body thinning out but still retaining a residue of little-girl plumpness.

"You tired?"

"I wish I had a horse," she said.

"Let's rest," Mike said with his eight-year-old's directness.

The children selected rocks on either side of the trail and sat.

"Horse," David said. "Are you still on that horse kick?"

Carol drank from her canteen. "I'd take care of it," she said solemnly. "Feed it."

"Living on a mountaintop is not the same as living on a farm," David said. He pulled a flashlight out of one hip pocket and a half-full bottle of beer out of the other. He used his thumb to remove the pressed-back-on cap. He sat drinking the beer and looking out into the mountain forest. Red and white oaks, hickory, and sweet gum trees provided a lush canopy of June foliage over their heads. The earth smelled dank and musty from a recent rain.

It won't carry me, he thought. I should've brought the flask.

But Grace had been worried, worried, worried, as usual. "Surely you don't need to drink on a hike with the children."

He didn't bother to remind her that his drinking was deliberate, calculated, and always under control when he wanted it to be. It's no worse than any number of other things that we bribe our senses with in an effort to make life more bearable. Why don't we give them all up: coffee, cigarettes, rich foods . . . copulation?

"We could keep it in the garage in the winter-time," Carol said. "When you build it, I mean."

David glanced sharply at her to see if he could detect any hint of innuendo in the "when you build it."

Her face was solemnly inscrutable.

I wouldn't put it past her, he thought.

If he had slowed down in his initially ambitious house-building project, it was because every human machine must slow down as it approaches its death. He was on the brink of forty, not a golden thirty-two as he had been when he had started the project. He was flat tired, and the spirit of adventure and personal accomplishment in the beginning had given way to a drudgery that he found increasingly diffi-cult to force himself to.

"Horse," he muttered. "Carol, every twelve-year-old girl in the world wants a horse. It's tied in with their sexual development."

"Daddy," she said evenly, "I just want a horse."

"What's 'sexy devilment'?" said Mike, chewing a leaf.

David laughed. "Good paraphrasing, boy."

"You wouldn't understand," Carol said quietly.

"I don't," he replied. "What's 'parapraising'?"

At Flint Arsenal, in the valley and beyond the town, a static test rocket rumbled. David listened, automatically counting off seconds, trying to deter-mine which one it was. The sound ended abruptly.

132

He shrugged. Whatever it was it didn't blow up.

A deep silence enfolded them. Not even the buzz of a cricket was to be heard. The children appeared to be awed by it, cutting their large children's eyes slowly from side to side as they drank from their canteens.

David arose, shoving the flashlight back into his pocket and pitching the empty beer bottle into a clump of bushes. He belched, wryly twisting his face at the memory of a rebellious stomach. "We'd better get going if we want to see this hole in the ground."

They started down the trail again. His mind turned to things he *should be* doing—like installing the kitchen cabinet doors. Grace had been waiting six years, with her groceries showing. . . . Hell, I should be hiking with my daughter and son; I haven't got around to that either. I can't remember the last time, or even if there was a last time. First too busy, then too tired.

He thought again of the left-behind flask—instant energy, instant optimism, fountain of youth. He wished fervently for a good, stiff, optimistic drink of deliberately calculated bourbon.

The trail took a sharp turn to the left, becoming steeper. At the end of the turn Bottomless Well came into view. David saw that there were the remains of a barbed-wire fence around the site and, nearby, a small stone house that the CCC had built, so he had heard, back in the thirties. There once had been plans to build an access road to the site and make it a public attraction. The plans had for some reason fallen through, and only the fading ghosts of human meddling remained.

The opening of the well proper, essentially a vertical-running cave, was at the center of a large depression in the ground, a sinkhole. There was an old theory that the well extended all the way down through the mountain and connected with great limestone caverns under the town of Garth at the mountain's foot. In support of this theory was the legend of the duck that had been dropped into the hole, reappearing a week later, much ruffled but alive, at the bottom of the hill on which the town was built.

However, recent exploration by local spelunkers had failed to find the legendary passage, and they had dryly reported its bottom to be some three hundred feet into the rocky bowels of Buena Vista Mountain.

David extended his arms in warning as they approached the funnel-shaped depression. The walls of the funnel descended at a forty-five-degree angle to the dark opening of the well.

"Take it very easy," he said. He had forgotten what a treacherous thing this hole in the ground was. The mouth of the crater was roughly circular and perhaps sixty feet across. The well opening at its bottom was more irregular in shape and about twenty feet across at its widest point. Someone had rolled a hickory log across the opening—not too long ago, judging by its sound appearance. David guessed that the log had been a part of the spelunking activity; certainly without it it would be hard to imagine what they would have secured a line to. Other evidence of activity at the site was a set of crude dug-out steps leading down the earth bank of the funnel to the near end of the log.

David picked up a small stone and pitched it toward the opening. After a prolonged silence, there was a faint *clink,* another silence, then another *clink;* after that it was difficult to tell whether you heard anything or not.

"Moses!" Mike whispered. "It must be a thousand feet deep!"

"Bottomless," Carol said.

David glanced at her, wondering at the solemnity of this little person he had sired. He could never help suspecting a precocious sardonicism, or at least satire, in her consistently restrained manner and speech.

"The folks who went down there say it's about three hundred feet." David addressed the remark to Mike. "Down. Then a short tunnel to the side."

"The length of a football field," Carol said, as if to herself.

"I'll take you down," David said, "but one at a time. I couldn't watch both of you at once." He gazed at them, almost selecting Mike first out of spite. "You first, Carol."

"All right."

"Mike," David said, "you stand *right there*. Don't you move until we come back up."

"Yessir."

They had to duck through the barbed wire to get to the steps leading down. David went first, keeping his body low and backleaning, insisting that Carol do the same. At the log they stopped and cautiously peered over into the chasm with their hands on the end of the log for support. The walls of the hole, though generally sheer, were broken at irregular intervals by narrow, rounded ledges of stone. The flashlight beam was able to probe only a feeble distance into the darkness. David picked up a pebble and tried to direct it so that it would miss the ledges and free fall as far as possible. As he let it go, he counted, "One thousand one, one thousand two. . . ." He heard a *clink* after about a three-second count. He struggled with some mental arithmetic and discovered, to his irritation, that he had forgotten how to figure it. Rotting inwards and mossy brained. It would be difficult to convince anyone that I was ever a paratrooper or that I'm supposed to be an engineer. I don't know that I could convince myself, he thought.

For Carol's benefit he muttered a guess. "Hundred feet maybe. There must be a prominent ledge at about that level."

She gazed solemnly and silently into the blackness of the hole.

He tried other trajectories and finally counted better than four seconds before the first sound, this time a distant splash.

"About two hundred and seventy or eighty feet, if you disregard drag," Carol said, after a moment of silence.

Drag, schmag! Shades of the space age! Yet he could not help feeling an obscure admiration for her, maybe even pride.

"I think we still haven't reached bottom," David said.

"That's possible," Carol said gravely.

"Would you like to try?"

"All right."

She tried several times, but her throwing arm was not as good as her physics.

"Let's let Michael," she said finally.

He was in the process of turning when he heard the sodden cracking of rotten wood and Mike's sharp cry. The fence post that he had been leaning against had suddenly snapped, and Mike was plunging down the steep side of the funnel six feet to one side of where David and Carol were crouched.

Instantly David launched his body in a horizontal line of motion, striking dank earth flat-out, skidding across and down, even in this paroxysm of motion outraged, thinking, My God, I might have known he'd do that. His hands clutched at the earth and closed on tenuous sassafras roots. His motion stopped coincident with the impact of Mike's body

137

from above. His own body shifted downward with the impact, and in slow, creeping motion moved to within inches of the brink of the well. His face pressed into the earth, and his body felt so poised on the edge of further movement that he wondered if he dared speak.

He tried it. "Mike?"

"Dad?"

He could feel the trembling in Mike's body, hear it in his hushed voice. "Get hold of something, boy."

"I'm scared to move."

"Move real slow. Get hold of a root."

"I can't. . . ."

"*Do* it!"

"Dad." Carol spoke as if in the imminence of a snake's strike. "You're mighty close to the hole, Dad."

"I know, I know. I know that. Get a stick, Carol. A strong one. Long enough. Hurry!"

He heard her quick steps up the side of the funnel, soon after heard the snapping of a branch up above. At least I can depend on her not to get a rotten one.

He felt the slightest shifting of the earth beneath him. "Hurry, Carol!" He still did not dare try to move his head in an attempt to look for her.

"I'm here," she said after a moment.

"Brace yourself good on the log and reach out with the stick so Mike can grab it."

"All right. . . . Here, Mike. *Grab!*"

"I . . . can't," Mike said. "I'm scared. . . . Dad?"

"Do it, Mike. You've got to do it." He felt a slight, tentative movement as Mike extended a hand toward the stick.

"All right," he heard Carol say. "Now the other hand . . . slowly. . . . Got it?"

He felt Mike nod, then felt the boy's weight slowly coming off his body.

"I've got you," Carol said. "You dig your feet in as best you can, and I'll do the pulling."

He felt Mike's body complete its departure from his, and simultaneously the strained damp earth released from the underlying rock and David went over the chasm's brink in a twisting, arching motion, then falling feet down and spread eagle. He hit the first ledge in approximately this attitude but leaning slightly forward so the impact was distributed fairly evenly along his thighs, belly, chest, and the undersurfaces of his arms. He hit clawing and scrabbling for a purchase on the damp stone. He pressed his body to the stone and felt the final momentum of his fall come to a slithering, tenuous halt on the rounded contour of the ledge. It was only when his motion stopped that he was aware of the shrill screams from above.

In his delicate balance on the ledge he couldn't bring himself to use his lungs, from which most of the air had been forced by his flat impact against the stone. Then he could not forestall the reflex any longer. In a raucous inhalation he sucked in air and felt a slight downward shift of his body. He dug his fingernails into the stone, bringing the slithering motion to another perilous halt. His feet in this last movement had left the rock and projected out over the chasm below. His hands had found some small cross-running ridges in the stone, but his fingers already had begun to ache, all the strength of his body, it seemed, concentrated at their stiffened tips.

"Daddy! Daddy! Oh, Daddy, Daddy!"

He recognized through his stunned senses the terror-stricken voice of Carol. He steeled himself for an answering call. He didn't know whether or not he could talk at all, or, if he did, whether he could do so without destroying his pitiful purchase on the ledge.

"Daddy!"

Now he could distinguish both their voices, and with that he had his first real knowledge that Mike had not fallen too. It at least gave his plight some meaning. He imagined them crawling out on the log or venturing upon the treacherous slope of the funnel in an effort to see him.

"Carol," he said in a hoarse whisper. His fingers remained clamped to the stone. "Mike? Can you hear me?"

"Yes, Daddy. Yes." They, too, were whispering, as if they were as aware as he was of his delicate balance on the ledge.

"Carol, don't endanger yourselves. I'm all right.

But . . . listen, honey, Mike, I'm going to need help. Fast as you can."

I don't know, I don't. . . . I couldn't possibly hang on long enough.

"Mike?"

"Yes, Daddy?"

"Mike, do you think you could find your way home?"

"Yessir! I'll . . . find it."

"Listen carefully, boy. Tell Mother to call the spelunkers."

"Cave explorers," he heard Carol say.

"Yes. Tell them your daddy. . . . Tell them I'm in a deep hole—Bottomless Well. They know about it. Need rope, climbing equipment."

"Yessir." His voice sounded steady enough under the circumstances.

"Daddy," Carol said. "I can see you. Can you hang on?"

"I don't . . . I don't know. . . . Mike, you hurry. Follow the path. . . . Carol, you stay here with me?"

"Yes, Daddy, I won't leave."

"Go now, Mike. . . ."

"Yessir!" His voice was already receding.

"Carol?"

"Yes, Daddy?"

"Is Mike gone? . . . Tell him to take care and tell him . . . tell him . . . that I love him."

"All right, Dad—" Her voice broke off abruptly.

141

My God, have they heard it from me so seldom?

He thought he felt a slight creeping of his body on the stone and made a special effort to check his handhold, looking carefully at each of his fingers in turn. His hands looked spatulate and froglike on the rock, the tendons showing through flesh like taut cables. Oddly, he was not afraid, at least at that moment he wasn't. He felt a profound animal alertness the like of which he couldn't remember having felt since his combat days. He also felt the beginning of a kind of tender sadness that he would have found impossible to define.

In the waiting silence he took time to try to assay his position—and his chances of survival. At least as a paratrooper, he thought wryly, I've had some training and experience in the business of falling. It's not as new to me as a lot of other things are. He calculated, from the feel of the fall and from an educated guess as to which of the preobserved shelves of rock he had hit, that he had fallen twenty or thirty feet. He was most certainly bruised and abraded, but, as far as he could tell, unbroken— except maybe for a cracked rib or two. With a keen inner ear he tried to plumb the sounds and feelings of his insides, but he could not penetrate the numbness.

He turned his thought to the almost inevitable *next* fall. Movement upward to a safer and less demanding perch was unthinkable; his first effort would certainly send him plunging again. And yet he was certain, too, that he could not hang on for the hour or maybe two that it would take for help to come. . . . That is, if it came at all. It was his sad admission that he did not know how much trust he could place in Mike, because he had not, as far as he could recall, ever before tested his trustworthiness.

He was suddenly aware of motion on the rock. Focusing his eyes, he saw that it was a small spotted salamander waddling by not three inches from the end of his nose. Fascinated, he watched its progress across the ledge. To the salamander this stone, in this hole in the ground, was a native dwelling, a place where all the vital functions of life were carried out. Here in its home, he, David Masters, Homo sapiens of sorts, waged a ludicrous war of survival —an injured, out-of-place animal, clumsy, clinging with desperation to the alien rock.

I wonder how the salamander would do in my world? No worse than I have—ill adapted, sick at heart, desperately clinging to unsubstantial things like self-pity, infidelity . . . alcoholism. Yes, I'm that too; I would have called it any word but that, but that's what I am.

He felt the slightest giving of his body on the stone—a concession to gravity, a low coefficient of friction and fatigue. He tightened his fingers.

It would be nice to know what's directly below, he thought. I don't remember, or the light didn't shine down that far.

143

He thought of the flashlight in his hip pocket. Go ahead, Dave boy, pull it out and shine it down there where you're gonna be. Enlighten yourself. Go ahead.

He clutched the stone, letting the first wave of hysteria wash over him, and then, recognizing it, putting it aside for the moment.

Perhaps a lucky fall and a kinder ledge down there? . . . Or death. He let himself think about that rationally. Why not? He'd already accepted it. He'd been killing himself for years. The stone could be no less kind in its infliction of death. In fact, it undoubtedly would be more merciful, certainly without rancor. . . . Let go, you idiot! You'll never have a better chance.

"Daddy?"

He curved his aching fingers into the unyielding stone.

"Yes, Carol?"

"I've got a grapevine. I'm going to let it down and swing it over to you."

"Honey, honey. . . . Carol. . . ."

"It's very strong, Daddy. I had to chop it off at the bottom with a sharp rock."

"Carol. . . ."

"Daddy, I'm letting it down. You'll feel it touch your back in a minute."

Tears flowed from his eyes and salted the stone under his cheek. He tried to look up but couldn't

144

complete the effort. He felt something brush his right shoulder like a warm caress.

"Carol—" He choked on the word. "Honey, how have you got it tied?"

"I tried to tie it around the log, Daddy, but it's too thick; I can't bend it enough."

"Carol, honey, don't bother, don't—"

"Daddy, I've got my legs wrapped around the log. I can hold it, I can."

"No, Carol, darling. I'd just pull *you* in. Besides, you couldn't possibly pull me up."

"I could hold you till they come."

He tried to stifle his free-flowing tears. If only I could give my life meaningfully for her, he thought with hopeless regret.

"No, Carol. I don't think I could let go to reach for it anyhow. Now you pull it on back up, honey."

It seemed he could *feel* the vine receding from him, and it made him feel infinitely lonely.

"Carol?"

"Yes?" He could hear the helpless defeat in her voice.

"Thank you, darling. . . . I love you." It was getting easier to say.

Unexpectedly, as if he had been struck a sudden blow from above, his grip failed. He slid off the ledge and fell, essentially in the spread-eagle attitude of his earlier fall. He had no time to resign himself to anything before his extended leg smashed into merciless stone. He hit differently this time, less flat, taking a large part of the impact on one leg; sharp pain in that leg informed him, too, that he had hit with more damage to himself than before. But again, before sliding over the new precipice, he flattened himself to the rock and brought his motion to a stop. His purchase was somewhat better, more secure than before, but his strength had been greatly sapped by his previous effort.

"Daddeeeeee!" He heard the wail from above, profoundly regretting the ordeal of terror he was inflicting on her. He laboriously sucked air into his lungs.

"Carol. I'm . . . all right, honey. I'm on another ledge. I . . . might be able to hang on."

"Daddy, I can't see you anymore!"

"I know. Much darker. . . ."

So this is the way it ends. Maybe befitting enough, swallowed up by the mountain he loved. . . . Determined he had been to return to gentle Garth and its magnificent mountain, Buena Vista, and on an expansive wooded lot build a fine house with his own two hands and his native intelligence—a house with a fieldstone fireplace big enough to warm a man's soul, and massive oak beams, like security itself, overhead. Then live an active, creative, meaningful life, full of good cheer, with Grace, and with the most wondrous children of their flesh. . . .

And they lived happily never after.

146

"Daddy?"

He had to think a moment, then gather himself.

"*Daddy!*"

"Yes, yes, Carol. I'm here."

"Oh." A silence. "Daddy, will you say something every now and then, so I'll know you're all right?"

"Yes, honey. I'm sorry. Every minute I'll tell you I love you. Okay?"

"Oh, Daddy, Daddy. I feel so *bad*."

He thought he felt something splash down upon him and momentarily clung to the belief that it was her tears. It was as if she had touched him, and he felt less lonely.

He let a delirium wash over him.

Ah, such golden dreams! But he pooped out, got diverted and perverted, overly involved with failure and preoccupied with advancing years, blighted with cynicism, infidelity, mistrust, and nuclearitis. At least I built, I mean completed, the fallout shelter. I finished it, no doubt, because it sickened me. It's typical of my recent attitude and behavior. . . .

"I love you, Carol," he called up to her.

"I love you, Daddy," she called back.

If we love each other, why haven't we shown it? What have we been doing all this time? . . .

A far cry, David, from the golden man with his golden dream. Where did the degenerative process start? Who knows? . . . It seemed that cause and effect were lost in a hopeless tangle of nega-

147

tiveness. Golden man, after two wars and much searching, returns to Garth with his golden wife to work at the thing he had been trained to do: engineering. Maybe that was it; maybe there had been too many years and too many other things between the learning and the doing. Maybe some obscure incident he couldn't even remember had conveyed that to him and started a chain reaction of doubt. At any rate, he had failed to secure the feeling of competence and of being respected in his profession. And the lack of those things, which had been a basic part of his plan and a basic part of his need, could have started a pattern of defeat in him that he could never overcome.

And Garth. What had happened to his beloved Garth? No longer quiet, no longer a sleepy Southern town, no longer the embodiment of a boyhood memory. It was not even *called* Garth anymore, but names like Space City and Rocketville, USA. Not a town at all anymore, but a madhouse of bustle and outrageous growth and profit and spoilage.

At least that was the way he had looked at it, even if it and its missile business, its dynamic Flint Arsenal, *had* provided him with the means to return.

Man oh man! I could use a drink.

As he pressed his life-worn flesh to the deathless stone, he thought in another flash of hysteria, Wouldn't it be something if I, needing a drink now maybe for the first time in my life, really needing it, had the flask, miraculously unbroken in my hip pocket . . . and not being able to get to it. Needing it just like I need that flashlight and both of them a million miles away on my butt. A perverse laughter bubbled in him.

The next fall caught him almost unaware of its occurrence. In midair, as he sank again into the abyss, realization struck him, and instinctively he made an effort to control the attitude of his body. He hit jarringly on his legs and his right hip and sank wearily into a broken heap on the new ledge. His senses were dulled almost beyond physical pain, and in one sense he was filled with a fatal hopelessness; yet as he felt himself slipping once again over an inevitable brink he clutched the impersonally sadistic rock and, momentarily at least, found a purchase.

Through his shocked sense he listened for sounds from above. Thank God. I don't believe she even knew about that one.

"Carol?" His voice floated up through the tube of stone.

"Yes, Daddy." Her voice sounded small and weary, weary beyond her age.

"Carol . . . it is perfectly natural for a girl of any age to . . . to want a horse."

"Daddy . . . don't—"

"You're a good girl, a good person, Carol. You ask for little. You'll have your horse. . . . Tell Mother—"

His senses blackened, and with infinite sadness

and regret he slid off into his waiting void, even in his delirious exhaustion clutching for some useful and substantial handhold, and then, not finding it, falling, trying to orient his plunging body into some rightful order of descent.

He opened his eyes to a spot of light directly above; bending into the light was a hallucination, then another.

Sudden memory signaled a sharp warning to his brain, spurted adrenalin into his veins. His arms moved like pistons, hands clutching at stone. They found no substance, and he knew he was falling again. His body twisted in an effort to gain the proper attitude of falling; sharp pains shot through his legs.

"He's conscious, Ben. Help me hold him."

Reality returned to his brain and, more slowly, to the desperate reflexes of his body.

Conscious? Conscious of what? . . . Oh, yes. . . .

He felt firm hands restraining his arms.

"It's all right, fella. Just take it easy."

In one arm he felt the distant prick of a needle. He looked up at the owner of the voice, a bespectacled face loosely attached to a small, wiry body. He slowly let out his taut breath. "So . . . I finally stopped falling." His voice sounded hollow and hardly recognizable as his own.

"You did. It's a fairly broad shelf. Covered with several inches of silt, luckily for you."

Another face leaned out of the shadows. "My hat's off to you, mister. It's bad enough coming down here on a rope. You must be living right."

In a distant corner of his mind David heard the ring of ironic laughter.

The bespectacled man, apparently a doctor, listened to his chest with a stethoscope. He nodded. "We'll hoist you up now."

"My family? Grace?"

"They're up there."

His memory leaped. "Mike?"

The doctor chuckled. "You mean the new sprint champion of Tuscahatchee County? I don't believe a Sherman tank could remove him."

David and the doctor gazed at each other.

"You're pretty busted up, but as far as I can tell there's nothing we can't patch."

David looked up at the rough circle of daylight above him. He felt an old identity flowing into him like the return of a benevolent ghost.

"Doctor," he said, smiling with a new inner bearing that was at once profound and risible, "what's it like on the outside?"

The man smiled back at him. "You'll soon be finding out."

"Doctor," David said, "you can say that again."

The Virgin Cave

BRYCE WALTON

Professor Ernest Albracht fussed with the winch motor over the cave opening while his favorite graduate student, Gerard Middleton, finished unloading the jeep. Then Gerard, with careful efficiency, began filling up three haversacks with equipment and supplies for the big drop. He continued to move with an apparent easy calm, but he wondered how long he could bear the strain of waiting.

Nylon sleeping bags. Flashlights. Butane stove kits. Portable ladders. Hammers. Acetylene lamps. K rations. . . .

Gerard frowned. He wished Ellen wouldn't sit over there in the shade that way, smugly watching and singing. Albracht must not, of course, suspect anything, so they had to act natural. But Ellen shouldn't sing. She shouldn't act happy about what would soon happen to Albracht. She must have had some love or respect for him once; she had married him.

"Shake it up, Gerard," Albracht said in his kindly voice, as soothing as a doctor's. "This day'll be a scorcher, but nature's finest air conditioning awaits us below."

Gerard smiled dutifully. He avoided looking at Ellen, who kept sitting over there, singing in the shade of eroded rock and wild cucumber vines. Gerard didn't have to look at her. He saw her with his eyes closed. But he couldn't stand looking and not being able to touch her whenever he pleased. Because of Albracht, of course. He had to control himself a while longer. Then Albracht wouldn't be around. Never be around again.

Albracht had said he'd seen a small hole in the rocks no bigger than a varmint hole. He'd stuck his walking stick in, and the hole crumbled away to reveal a virgin cave. Now the opening was four feet wide. A winch had been built over the hillside hole, for they had to make a 600-foot drop by cable. A gray, taciturn hillbilly named Landaff was hired to stay topside and handle the winch motor. Albracht was helping him fuss with an ornery carburetor.

Gerard felt a sudden chilling burst of sweat as the motor abruptly kicked loose, then kept pounding away in a steady, dependable rhythm. He took a deep breath, then hooked the haversacks to the winch cable, and, as Landaff prepared to lower them one by one, he joined Albracht and Ellen in the ritual of putting on appropriate clothing for the drop. Woolen shirts and socks, spike-soled boots, rubberized suits, spun-glass helmets with headlamps attached, and earphones with attached microphones.

No one said anything. They had to keep acting natural. Gerard usually avoided talk, while the Albrachts had given up trying to communicate with each other years ago.

Albracht clipped his webbed shoulder harness to the cable hook, slid down, and watched the lever controlling the cable spool until he was supported entirely by the creaking wire. Landaff revved up the motor.

Gerard and Ellen smiled down at the professor. The professor, pink-faced with boyish excitement, his graying hair fluttering slightly, smiled up at them around his pipe stem, then suddenly sank out of sight into the earth.

Landaff squatted by the winch motor watching them, so Ellen and Gerard avoided intimate glances. She was lowered next.

Gerard felt heat building up inside his rubberized suit. It had been a long wait. But then, when he was being lowered after Ellen, he realized that he hadn't really allowed himself to feel the accumulated tensions before.

The cozy secret meetings with Ellen, the exciting, dangerous whispering and planning—all of it suddenly exploded like one of his beautiful daydream bubbles. A chilling reality closed in around him as cold and black as a grave.

He could go through with it. He had to. But something seemed to be wrong with his face. He had lost control of it. He knew that his expression wasn't right. The comfortable, safe old mask had slipped off. It might even look real, he thought, the way he actually felt inside. Albracht mustn't see that. He might become suspicious.

Gerard worked on his face all the way down into the chilling darkness. He fitted the old safe mask back on, the one that never showed anything.

Later their headlamps made three tiny, stifled glimmers of light in a vast and absolute blackness as they half slid, single file, down a high shale hill. Albracht took the lead. Gerard followed Ellen.

"This haversack hurts my shoulders," Ellen said. "Is all this boy-scout equipment really necessary?"

"Yes," Albracht said. "It's all necessary. Caving is a dangerous sport. The loss of any item in your haversack could mean your death down here."

"You know a better way?" Ellen said, and giggled.

You shouldn't do that, Gerard thought. For you it's natural, but under present circumstances it isn't right; it's in bad taste.

As they explored along, Albracht stuck strips of

red phosphorescent plastic tape to rocks. If necessary, it would guide them back in total darkness to the winch cable. It would lead rescuers to them in case of trouble, to any one of them. Just another thing Gerard had to keep in mind. It must happen in such a way that rescue would be impossible. If he botched this, he could hardly expect a second chance.

Although it must be done without a hitch, it was impossible to figure the exact method in advance—not in a virgin cave. But there were a number of excellent possibilities. A person could be crushed by a falling rock, pinned down to expire slowly; fall down a rocky shelf; get stuck in a fissure or crevice; fall into a bottomless pit; freeze, drown, or get lost; or be sucked into an underground river's flume. A person might build a fire in a cavern that had insufficient fresh oxygen and die from carbon monoxide poisoning. Cave deaths have even resulted from untimely explosions of bat guano.

All these possibilities shared a common virtue—they appeared accidental. Ellen had taken out two double-indemnity policies on Albracht.

So he must stay alert, ready to seize exactly the right moment and select exactly the right place, and then act with pan-flash decision.

Ellen stopped suddenly. Gerard bumped into her and felt his stomach twitch as Albracht yelled up at them. He yelled again through megaphoned hands, this time in all directions. Measuring the cave's size, he explained, by timing the returning echoes of his voice. Then he said very quietly, "Seems to be a tremendous cavern. A real find."

"Congratulations," Gerard said.

"It always gets to me," Albracht said. "The feeling that no one's been here before you."

"Why should anybody ever be here?" Ellen said. "Why would anyone rather be a mole than a man?"

"So let me suggest again, most sincerely, my dear"—somehow Albracht maintained a gentle tolerance—"that you go back up and wait for us."

"One thing is more boring than crawling about in a hole," Ellen said. "Being alone in an Ozark cabin on a hot summer day."

"You never minded before."

"The television worked."

But Gerard knew the real reason she had insisted on making this drop—to be sure he did the job, and did it properly.

"A tremendous erosion pocket," Albracht said. "Seems cathedral size."

"They'll name it after you, dear," Ellen said. "You'll be immortal. I can see it now—Ernie's Hole."

Albracht moved on without comment, his body a gesture of tireless forebearance. He managed skillfully to find ways through boulders and stalagmites. But it seemed to Gerard, depressingly, that they only made a large, erratic circle without finding another exit. Still there has to be one, Gerard thought, his mouth dry. It had to happen to Albracht in some remote cavern or labyrinth, not here where Landaff would know at once if there was trouble.

Albracht sank to his knees. He flashed his light into a small opening through a wall of sparkling limestone crystal. "Cold draft coming," he mused aloud. "Probably another cavern at the other end. Seems short, no more than fifteen feet, I'd say, judging from the sound of running water coming through. Might be a tight squeeze, so you may have to push your haversacks through ahead of you. I'll go first. If it's clear, I'll give you the word to follow." Albracht was still talking with boyish enthusiasm as he wriggled away out of sight.

Ellen gave Gerard a sly, conspiratorial wink. He smiled back, but slightly past her direct gaze, and found his sight going out into infinite blackness. He felt a quick, sharp squirm of fear.

Her whisper exploded in the vast stillness like a paper bag. "This caving is so childish and stupid!"

"So are a lot of things," Gerard said.

"But he hasn't really cared about anything else for years. Why?"

"I know facts," Gerard said. "You want to know how these erosion pockets are formed out of limestone? Okay, I can tell you. But—"

"You're already beginning to talk like a damn professor. Like *him*!"

Albracht's sudden sepulchral voice came out of the rock. "All right now, Ellie. It's about twenty feet. Careful."

She smiled at Gerard, then squirmed out of sight. He shivered. It wasn't just her eyes or her smile. Whatever she said, the way she stood or sat or walked, was an invitation and a promise. . . .

He had been most grateful for her smile. At first, he had been grateful only to Albracht. The professor taught botany and speleology, and the latter was also his hobby. When not lecturing or writing treatises and popular articles on caves, he explored them. Every summer he favored one graduate student with an invitation to share the Albrachts' vacation in their Ozark cabin. Relaxation was combined with speleological field work around Lake Tanacomo.

Albracht had first invited Gerard to his house near the campus to share a faculty tea. Gerard had been deeply grateful for Albracht's recognition. He met Ellen that afternoon, and she smiled at him. Few women had ever smiled at Gerard, and none had ever smiled at him quite that way. In all his life no woman like Ellen had ever really looked at him. Attractive, sophisticated, much younger than Albracht, who was fifty, Ellen had a genuinely hypnotic charm.

Gerard's gratitude was measureless. Too many of his twenty-five years had been fevered away during lonely nights with books, ambitions, and dreams instead of human beings. Too many years alone, quietly bitter, secretly angry for always having to work his way, he had every reason to be a bottomless well of gratitude. Grateful for Albracht. Grateful for Ellen and her smile. Indescribably grateful for what came after the smile during those secret cozy meetings. Most grateful for her promises. Gerard had been hungry all his life.

They stood on a dangerously narrow ledge about twelve feet long. And Albracht studied the rent in Ellen's rubberized suit made by snagging rock. Ellen's face was pale. In the beam of Albracht's headlamp the gash in her suit looked like a jagged, perhaps mortal wound.

Albracht kept insisting that Ellen turn back at once because of the torn suit. But Ellen insisted on continuing what she called "this most fabulous exploration of the century." Gerard caught part of a supposedly clever remark about her being a beautiful icicle or the greatest of all tourist attractions, a stalagmite shaped like a girl.

But Gerard was more concerned with the sound of the river gurgling below. The beam of his headlamp caught the water's dark shine swirling deep and deadly through ice-coated rocks. It can happen here, he thought, here and now. Albracht could fall into the river. No, it must be absolutely certain. Albracht could fall into the river, but only if it was certain he would drown.

Ellen leaned toward Gerard. "What's that chirping?"

Gerard moved his flash and focused it in a tiny crack. "Cave cricket."

"What was that, young man?" Albracht asked, assuming a deliberately exaggerated professorial tone.

"*Ceuthopilus*, sir," Gerard said in mock apology. "Similar to the cricket found in cellars. After a few generations born in total darkness, their eyes become useless and are bred out. They also lose their color. No need of protective camouflage in total darkness."

"Very good," Albracht said. "Yes, my favorite pupil."

"Mine, too," Ellen said. "But that awful cricket. I hate it. White like a little slug and with no eyes."

"But it's happy without light," Albracht said. "It loves and lives and sings."

"It shouldn't," Ellen said. "It shouldn't want to sing or be alive here at all."

She stepped back in disgust and would have fallen from the ledge if Albracht hadn't caught hold of her. But she let out a high, sharp yell. It disturbed thousand of bats hibernating somewhere up in the darkness.

Albracht shouted a warning. Gerard covered his eyes with his arms as a hot, stinking mass squealed around him. He remembered that cave bats' teeth were usually not strong enough to break skin, and they used their sonar to fly, so they were never likely to get in your hair. But they could take out your eyes.

Gerard uncovered his eyes at Ellen's second scream. He saw her topple backward into the misty blackness as the last of the bats fluttered away. Her headlamp and helmet flew off, and when the light left her, her body seemed to dissolve in a black paste. It fell in a strangely stiff way except for her arms that went round and round twice like pale lily stalks. Then she toppled end over end, as rigid as a display-window mannequin.

Albracht shouted. Gerard felt paralyzed with the horror of feeling his mask of control slipping. But he didn't lose control. The mask remained—the thin boyish look, diffident and shy, the wide and guileless blue eyes, the odd lack of animation.

He ran to help Albracht. He lunged out of fear and in an agony of release at the thought of Ellen dissolving into nothing. It was as if a spear had been jerked out of his pierced belly.

He got out the portable ladder—nylon cord with aluminum rings attached. He got the cord hooked to a spike, and the spike hammered into a crack below the ledge. Albracht climbed fearlessly down the ladder and plunged to his armpits in the vicious current. He slipped, went under, reappeared, spun away, and then clung helplessly to a rock.

162

Gerard got there fast, but he was frightened now. If Ellen was really gone, he'd be alone with it, alone in the darkness. The current dragged at him. But he was still in control, going slow, testing his spike soles on the slick bottom. He knew now that they were all an eyewink away from death.

As he worked along toward where Ellen's pale face and black hair bobbed like a matted cork, he saw, only thirty feet downstream, the river boiling suddenly down under a limestone wall in a seething whirlpool. Ellen was struggling weakly in a kind of backwash in the rocks. He finally managed to get the nylon line hooked to her webbed belt, and then Albracht helped him reel her into a large eroded pocket he had found in the limestone wall on a level with the rushing river.

There she sat shivering on a bed of fine gravel bleached as white as dried salt.

"Anything else wrong, Ellie? Broken bones or anything?"

Her blue lips worked until she finally stuttered faintly, "Just—just cold."

The icy water had entered through the tear in her suit, and she could freeze to death in minutes.

"We'll fix that up," Albracht said. "You'll warm up in the sleeping bag while we dry your clothes over the stove." He looked up at Gerard. "Get out the butane stove and set it up." Then he began unrolling Ellen's sleeping bag.

Gerard got the stove assembled, and as he lit it

163

he looked up. Something in his stomach turned completely over. Albracht was taking her clothes off. Gerard shivered, looked quickly away. He heard Albracht say, "Take a look over there where the river goes under the wall, Gerard, please. Maybe we can find a way through."

But Gerard didn't find a way through the wall. He worked back through the erosion pocket about fifty feet, but found no opening. He didn't want to find one. Albracht evidently wanted to keep on exploring if he found a way, but Gerard was finished. His nerves wouldn't stretch an inch farther.

He stood motionless in a forest of helectites, those stony formations that curl and twist in grotesque patterns. He saw through them to where, just beyond a thicket of icicles about thirty feet away, Ellen lay in the sleeping bag near the river. The scene was a weird frozen stillness, a small bowl of light locked in infinite blackness where nothing moved. Ellen didn't move. The propped flashlight was still and unblinking. No air stirred. The flame of the butane stove didn't flicker even slightly in the dead air.

And where was Albracht?

Gerard felt one of those recurring, engulfing needs to be with Ellen, to be close to her, as close as to his own body. When he'd been with her before, in that wondrous secrecy, she had made him feel heady, reckless, willing, and able to do anything.

164

He got to her as quickly as he could and knelt beside her sleeping bag. "Where's Albracht?"

Her little mocking smile had come back, but there was apprehension in her eyes as she pointed.

Gerard flashed his headlamp over through the rocks and listened

"You don't look so good," she said. "Better get on with it, before your feet get colder than mine."

Albracht's sudden shout jerked Gerard around and seemed to pinch at his stomach. Albracht's face, illuminated by his own flashlight, glowed suspended over the black water like a luminescent ceremonial mask. He was neck-deep in that treacherous tide, at the very edge of the whirlpool.

Ellen cried out in genuine disbelief. "Ernie, what are you doing there?"

Albracht yelled for the end of the nylon line. Gerard tossed it out. Albracht hooked it underwater to his belt "If I don't come back, haul me in," he said.

"What are you doing?" Ellen almost screamed.

"Don't worry," he shouted back, his face wet and shining with spray. "There's an airspace up here and if I don't slip I can get through without getting my face under. There's another big chamber on the other side of this wall. The river may come up again over there." He waved, and his head dissolved in foam. Then darkness.

* * *

Half an hour later Gerard still held the frayed broken end of the nylon line he had reeled in. There was still no sight or sound of Albracht.

"He must be crazy," Ellen whispered. "He wouldn't have that kind of nerve."

"Any caver has to have guts," Gerard said heavily. "Even him."

"But what's happened to him?"

"We don't know," Gerard said.

"We have to know."

"Yes. River might come up again over there, might not. Might have taken him down to hell."

"He must have thought he would come up somewhere."

"He must have. But he couldn't be sure."

"We have to make sure."

"We ought to," Gerard said.

"We have to *know* what's happened to him. He may be hurt. Broken bones, or something. He may still be alive. Maybe help can reach him. We don't *know*. Maybe he's all right and can get out some other way. We have to make sure."

"You mean *I* have to make sure." Gerard rubbed his hands together.

"Make sure he'll never be found, or not be found too soon."

Fear surged through Gerard's body. But it didn't show. He stood up. The fear was worse than other recent moments of near terror. But Ellen had enabled him to do what he could never have done anywhere else except in his dreams. And anything, any risk, was better than the dull, empty, unpromising loneliness he had always known before.

He hooked a nylon line to his belt, tied the other end around a stalagmite, and waded into the river.

"Wait for me here," he said. Then his spike-soled shoes slipped out into sickening softness, and the current dragged him down. A black mouth sucked and swallowed him. It chewed, it gurgled, it ground him down through a rocky gullet. He struggled like a helpless, futile bug flushed down a drain.

His webbed belt snagged. He kicked, he strained, he screamed inside, bursting and suffocating. His belt tore free, and he shot away and down, free of it, but leaving everything attached to it—knife, ax, first-aid kit, matches. Helmet and headlamp ripped away with some of his scalp. His tortured lungs, bursting, pried open his mouth. An icy paste of sooty black poured in to drown and freeze his soul.

He lay on corrugated rock somewhere near the river. He concentrated on maintaining control, his one dependable protection. Especially his breath. He kept his breathing low, slow, easy. If his breathing got loud, it echoed, and he would hear it even above the sound of the river. He didn't want to hear that again, not that loud, erratic blood thump in his ears. He didn't want to hear himself at all again. It was only a reminder of all the sound there was now or ever could be.

The river had spewed him up again, but there was no way of knowing where. A 600-foot drop, then a walk and a climb down several hundred feet, then the river had sucked him down. No way to figure how much farther down or to where.

There was no way out from wherever he was, no way but the river. He didn't want to make that terrible drop again. He could never bring himself to go that way again.

His shattered wristwatch was a phosphorescent smear on his arm. He had opened his eyes in pitch-blackness. There was no sound. Nothing turned. No light went off and on. Nothing stopped and started anywhere. There was no more time.

He knew he could have been wherever he was for hours, for weeks, for months. But he had no idea how long he could stay, how long he could keep himself alive.

He concentrated on holding himself in one rigid, integrated piece. The stillness was without end, the blackness absolute. He had bulged his eyes hopefully at first, strained and popped them at the dark, trying to find light somewhere, even the tiniest light. But pure blackness pressed over his face, muffled his nose and mouth, suffocated him.

He merely existed in the dark. A worm, he thought. A blind worm or one of the first amoebas that ever lived on earth.

He had hated his life. To change it into something else, anything else, he had been ready to kill a man.

A man whom he respected, a man who cared for him. But now the bitterest memory he had of that hated past was a vision of paradise. Sights, sounds, memories kept thumping at his brain, almost but never quite getting in, like bugs hitting lighted windows.

Now he could only lie blind and breathing in the dark. He had crawled in carefully measured circles, trying to find a way out. He had explored every inch, squirmed into every hole and over every rock. And he was sure now: there was no way out, no way but the river.

There were only little potholes, slightly warm from subterranean springs. Pools in which food bred, lived brief, blind cycles. Where salamanders crawled, totally blind, with layers of skin pulled by eons of evolution over the remnants of eyes they no longer needed.

Now Gerard felt blindly about. He grabbed, fumbled, lost, retrieved. The great blind hunter. He learned slyness and skill. Little crayfish, panarian worms, isopods, hydras, water sponges, even a few mollusks, slugs, and snails.

He caught and crushed them to watery pulp in his numbed fingers. He seemed to have eaten thousands of times, devoured thousands and thousands of salamanders, snails, slugs, crayfish—all as blind and white as he—but he knew that it would end sometime, that when he reached into the potholes and found them empty, found he had eaten them up faster than they could breed, it would be over. . . .

Slowly he opened his eyes. Silently he listened for that very tiny sound that had gone through him like a sliver of glass. Blackness. No change. He held his breath, waited, hoped. Only silence.

His gaze kept going out, meeting infinite layers of darkness. He started to raise his hand to his face, but there was no way to keep his eyes from seeing out and out into nothing.

He started to run.

His body thumped. It battered. It bounced and went down. Little violent explosions went off in his head—

But he was free now. Even if there were eyes here, the eyes of judges, juries, the condemning eyes of all his enemies, they couldn't harm him. They couldn't see his face to know how he felt, to know exactly where and how he was vulnerable. So they could never again attack, laugh, jeer, humiliate, beat, and murder him. He was safe now. No one ever again would see him exposed, naked, and helpless.

He had thought he was alone and safe before, hiding behind his expression, his perpetual mask. Now he knew what being alone really was. Oh, it was safe all right. And he knew something else— there were many things more horrible than being quite safe. No matter where you are, there is always a much worse place. No doubt of that. A much, much worse place.

He laughed.

Things seemed to break loose inside him. He began to yell, a monotonous, low, oddly controlled yelling as he beat the rocks with his fists. . . .

He kept grinning up at the light. He kept hoping it was a real light, a light that would never go away. He prayed. The light stayed, and, yes, that was the professor. Dear old Albracht! No mistaking that face shining under the headlamp's beam, that familiar, kindly face of Ernest Albracht.

The light stayed and shone down with that unearthly luminescence of angels seen in church windows. The professor's voice was gentle too, just like the touch of his hand reaching down, lifting up.

"Let's go now, Gerard. I'll help you."

Yes, sir, yes, sir. . . .

Albracht led the way without hesitation. He seemed to know exactly where he was and where he was going. But Gerard knew that he would never have the vaguest idea how they got through, through a maze that would have bewildered rats. Along narrow ledges, through narrow crevices, down shale slides, down slopes of fluted limestone, through tunnels of ice. . . .

When they got there, he knew at once where they were. He knew when Albracht started peeling off the phosphorescent strips of plastic tape. It was the route Albracht had once marked and was now dissolving behind them.

Gerard recognized the cathedrallike stillness, the

171

steep, high rockslide of glittering shale where the suspended cable gleamed like a strand of iridescent cobweb. And there was the cave opening 600 feet above his head. Gerard stood quivering below that bar of familiar light. It sliced down into his eyes, across his cheekbone and jaw, with a thin bar of fire.

He stumbled up the shale like a drunken mole in strong light. It was such a short way from where he had lain, where he had died over and over in the darkness. He just hadn't known the way. But Albracht knew. He seemed to have known all the time.

Gerard felt a cold charge of fear. Albracht's eyes were close to him now, like drops of clear, dark water, fixed and unblinking.

"This isn't a virgin cave," Gerard said. "You've been here before. You knew where we were going. You knew exactly where I was all the time."

"I've known about you and Ellen, too, for some time," Albracht said gently. "And I knew what you had planned for me." He took a slow drag at his pipe. "But let's go on up now, Gerard. We've got to break the news of the tragic accident to Landaff."

"Accident?"

"Oh, yes. She fell into the river, remember? A search party will be down here inside an hour. We'll all do our best to find Ellie, of course, but no one ever will. No one knows where the river goes."

"We could—" Gerard's voice broke.

"You think you could find her?" Albracht asked.

"No, believe me, you can't. No one can ever find her now."

"Why?" Gerard whispered. "Why have you saved me?"

"You're a fine scholar, Gerard, with a great potential to do good. I have always felt responsible to correct in what little ways I can the faults of miseducation."

Albracht smiled around his pipestem. "I left you there for seven hours, my boy, hoping it would bring about a vital change in you—for the better. As an experience, you know, a learning experience . . . a lesson for the future."

The Lost Continent

GEOFFREY HOUSEHOLD

Atlantis? It's of more interest to poets and mystics than to archaeologists. The lost continent is only a fable. We have no proof; you're looking at the best there is. No, not me. In the case behind my desk.

A puma, you think? Have you just been to the zoo? Well, then, why do you call it a puma? Yes, you're quite right. One could swear it was dug up in Peru or Ecuador. But an ivory puma is impossible. No pumas in the Old World. No elephants in the New World.

I'll tell you its history, though I warn you it is very unsatisfactory. It has no ending. You go out where you came in. You'll just say to hell with me and Jim Hawkes and all those visionary swordsmen who conquered the Americas and carefully destroyed or displaced every blessed thing they ought to have preserved for us.

But like all good stories it is really that of a man's character—a grubby little man with bad teeth and no education, who cared as little for money and as much for truth as any dedicated scholar rediscovering the past for the wages of a manual worker.

At first Jim Hawkes was not allowed in when he turned up at the side door of the museum and asked to see me. They thought he had samples in his little bag. That was what he looked like—a salesman peddling pens on commission. Yet there was something honest and earthy about him that was hard to distrust. He was a real Cockney, too, with the Londoner's genius for summing up doormen and minor officials and getting his own way in spite of them.

While he remembered to be on his best behavior he addressed me as "sir." When he got excited he called me "guv'nor." At that first interview he sensibly gave a thumbnail sketch of his background before coming to business, but I can't distinguish between what he said then and all I learned about him later. It's enough that he had passed twenty years of peace and war as steward on a tramp steamer, married a Portuguese wife, and settled down on her little farm in the Azores. He was one of those Englishmen who consciously loathe industrial civilization. Most of them haven't the enterprise to get out until they are tied to it. But Jim Hawkes knew an opportunity when he saw one. And the sea had already accustomed him to exile.

Introductions over, he asked me if I believed in Atlantis. He used the right word. It's a matter of belief, not scholarship. I told him gently that we believed in nothing without proof.

"Here it is," he said. He opened his bag, scattering straw all over the room, and put that ivory puma on my desk.

It was like nothing I had ever seen. So far as technique and material went it might have been a superb Persian ivory of the sixth or fifth century B.C., possibly brought to the Azores by the Carthaginians. But the style was wrong. Too realistic.

I remember thinking it odd that such a marvelous craftsman at carving ivory in the round had been unable to reproduce the strength and majesty of the lion. I know lions. In art, that is. Remind me to give you a copy of my monograph, *Treatment of the Conventional Mane*.

"It's not a lion," Jim Hawkes said. "I think it's a puma."

I made no comment. I took him across to the American Section and put his ivory alongside our two pre-Inca pumas—one in stone and one in pottery. Jim Hawkes had a case.

When we were sitting down again in my office, I asked him how he had got hold of such a curiosity,

rather suspecting that he would tell me some un-
believable yarn to cover up the fact that he hadn't
any right to it. But no. He was eager, falling over
himself to invite questions. That was why he had
come.

He told me that on the island of Graciosa he had
discovered a shallow cave with its entrance nearly
hidden beneath subtropical vegetation. The floor—
part earth, part fine, dry dust—was completely undisturbed. On a rock ledge at the back of the cave
was standing the ivory puma.

He thought at first it was a child's toy. For all I
know, it may have been, though an ivory a large as
a half-grown kitten argues a very high level of civilization in the nursery. Then he realized that it did
not belong to our day at all, and his mind at once
jumped to Atlantis.

But it would be wrong to think of him as just
one of those lost-continent-cum-flying-saucer sort of
cranks. His hobby—and I can't think of a better for
anyone living in the Azores—was Atlantis. He knew
all the usual arguments for and against. Like so
many seamen, he was a great reader, though he had
left school at the age of twelve. And he had a passion for facts. I tell you, he saw the difference between fact and conjecture much more clearly than
some of my colleagues.

"What I want, Mr. Penkivel, sir," he said, "is to
'ave that cave excavated proper like. Not treasure
'unting! Every cupful of soil sifted by them as knows

what's what. And I don't want nothink out of it for meself—and I'll pay the labor."

I asked him why me. Simple. He had turned up at the museum and demanded the bloke who knew most about ivories. Just possibly I am. But I also happened to be the bloke whom the porter was most annoyed with at the moment.

Now I really must repeat that there is no conclusive evidence for the existence of Atlantis. But as well as a so-called expert in ancient art, I am also a Cornishman. Part of us always dips into the ocean with the sun. So when I had taken Jim out to lunch next day and again convinced myself that he was dead straight, I decided I might as well spend the six weeks' holiday that was coming to me in running a trial trench through that cave. I did not tell my colleagues what I intended. They would have thought I needed a holiday even more than I really did.

Like all islanders Jim knew how to travel cheaply. When he returned to the Azores on a Portuguese cargo boat, I went with him, feeling self-consciously precious and wondering to what sort of society I had condemned myself.

I needn't have worried. Jim's background was in keeping with the man—simple and satisfying. He had a white, single-storied peasant house, three acres of wheat and pasture, and some terraces of fruit and vine, which wandered up the hillside. It was one of the highest farms on Graciosa, blazing with sun or hidden under blowing mist half a dozen times a day and looking out over a full semicircle of empty, secretive Atlantic.

All this he had married, together with Senhora Hawkes. It was certainly a love match, though it wouldn't have been possible without her inheritance. Maria Hawkes was a peasant poppet with the face of an angel and the body of Humpty Dumpty. She, too, had got a bargain by her marriage. Her energetic little ex-steward, always wanting to know why, had doubled the value of her land. They had as yet no children. That allowed Jim his luxury of Atlantis. His excuse for the journey to London had been a visit to his brother, but the senhora knew as well as I did that his true motive was to explain the ivory.

His cave was on a steep, overgrown hillside, high above their land. The entrance was a horizontal cleft under an overhang of rock, so that it could be seen only by a man climbing up from below, and even then he might not spot it through the bushes for what it was. Beyond the cleft was a roomy, low-roofed chamber, which ran back into the hill for seventy feet, narrowing all the way, until the passage ended at a fallen boulder.

It was just the sort of place to have sheltered early man. But the islands were uninhabited when the Portuguese discovered them, so I could not expect to find traces of anything larger than a rabbit. If I did, the historians and geographers would have a good deal of rewriting to do. That was a fascinating thought for a holiday, let alone the fact that I might come across another inexplicable ivory.

I don't normally dig; it's my job to give my opinion of what others have dug. But the cave would have been easy even for an amateur. Right inside, where Jim had made his find, there was only a layer of dust over the bedrock. We sifted all of this. It was quite sterile. I could trust him absolutely with the sieve. When I tell you that he managed to spot a rat's tooth, you can imagine how keen he was.

Over the rock at the entrance were eight feet of soil, shallowing rapidly, of course, as one got farther into the cave. Through this we drove our trench with the help of two laborers whom Jim had hired. Meanwhile, Maria Hawkes brought up enormous meals of fish and wine on a donkey and loaded the panniers with earth from our dig to put on her pineapples. She couldn't understand our professionally slow, patient progress. But if that was how her man wished to amuse himself she did not complain. Other wives had to put up with drink or gambling.

For the first week I was as happy as any fellow let out of an office can be. At the end of the second week I began to get bored. So did the onlookers, who left us for good. We found not a trace of man. The authorities are always right. A pity, except when I am the authority myself.

The only excitement came when one of our cross trenches hit charcoal only two feet above the bedrock. Jim Hawkes was bursting with expectancy and quite silent. He saw what it could mean. So did the laborers. But I had to tell them there was no evidence of a human hearth; it was undoubtedly blown debris from a forest fire. . . . I think I shall go out and look at it again.

Jim wouldn't let me pay for anything, and I knew he could not afford to go on. The farm was being neglected; ready money was short after his trip to London, and dear Maria Hawkes had added to the expense by considering it her duty to feed the spectators as well as us. At the end of the third week I persuaded Jim to give up and dismiss the laborers. I felt like . . . well, like a doctor telling him he must lose his leg. But it had become quite obvious that excavation was not going to tell us anything of the ivory puma.

When the first idle day was over—idle for me—I scrambled up to the cave and, of course, found Jim already there. He had been up before dawn and hoeing ever since, but now he was chipping away with a cold chisel at the boulder that blocked the end of the passage.

"Know anything about explosives, guv'?" he asked.

I said I did. Not a very likely trade for an antiquarian, but in the war I was a sapper.

"Then 'ow about it? Think we'd be muckin' up the evidence?"

Yes, that was what he said. He had the instincts of a born archaeologist.

181

I told him I was sure there was no evidence to muck up, but that the boulder would take some smashing. It had fallen from the roof recently. Say, two or three hundred years ago. To judge by the narrowing of the cave walls, I decided nothing much could be behind it, except a cleft or vent. That had to be there, for an occasional draft of warmish air could be felt at floor level. The air had removed my last faint doubt of Jim's story. It accounted for the preservation of the ivory, otherwise rather unlikely in the moist climate of the Azores.

There was a wide crack down the middle of the boulder and a useful cavity below it. Doubtfully I told Jim my requirements. They didn't bother him. He spoke very serviceable Portuguese and was popular everywhere. He was back the next evening with a keg of old-fashioned gunpowder—excellent stuff for shifting rock—from the island's general stores, this time on my bill, and had got fuse and detonators free from the whalers.

He did not mention what we were doing, even to Maria—most women are inclined to be excitable in the presence of explosives—so we had complete privacy. I made a good job of it, although my main length of fuse turned out to be a lot faster than the sample I had cut. I'm not sure whether I shot out of that cave together with the blast or just before it.

When the smoke had cleared, Jim and I opened up the passage. Fortunately, as it turned out, the whole force of the explosion had been directed outward, showering debris onto our working floor, cracking the rock, but disturbing nothing beyond it. We had still a couple of hours of work with pick and crowbar before we could reduce it to rubble and climb over.

To my surprise, the cave had done all the narrowing it was going to do and continued as a very rough V-shaped passage. I am not enough of a geologist to be sure of its origin. A combination of earthquake and steam pressure, I think.

Keeping the beams of our flashlights as much on the untrustworthy roof as on the ground, we cautiously followed the tunnel until it ended at an appalling abyss in the volcanic rock. That was where the warm air came from. A steam-heated hell fed by the tricklings-in at sea level or below. We threw down boulders and heard not the faintest sound. The gap was too wide to jump but fairly easy to bridge.

While I was wondering if I could ever pluck up enough courage to cross the homemade bridge that Jim—I knew it—was going to insist on constructing, he gave a shout. He was lying on his stomach, examining from a respectful distance the sheer edge of that terrifying drop. He pointed to what he had found. Two shallow grooves for the beams of a bridge had been chiseled out of the rock. Our flashlights showed two corresponding grooves on the opposite side of the chasm.

I have never been nearer to believing in a drowned continent. Who wouldn't in a place like that? I had quite unjustifiable visions of the very last of the inhabitants clinging to a barren peak, which later became the green island of Graciosa, and using the cave as their temple or treasure-house. Nothing impossible about the rock cutting. Atlanteans, if they existed, presumably had chisels of bronze or obsidian.

Oh, yes, I thought of that! I took some scrapings and dust home in an envelope. No trace of bronze or any metal at all. Not conclusive, but in favor of steel. Particles so tiny as those from a steel chisel would have been oxidized and blown away on a breath. The microscope did show a glassy dust like a form of obsidian, but even my Cornish blood refuses to build on that. A thousand to one that it was a natural component of the rock.

Farm work went overboard again. Serious, this time. There was a sudden squall from the south, which laid the heavy, overripe wheat. Maria wept, but Jim damned the weather and continued to square the ends of two twenty-foot lengths of pine sapling with a shipbuilder's adz so that they would fit the channels. Onto these spars we nailed planks from the bottom of an old farm cart. The donkey was busy all day, hauling timber up the slope.

By the next evening our bridge was ready. I don't believe we would ever have thrown it across the gap if not for Maria. She had a marvelous head for heights and just laughed at her husband, whose distaste for this beastly brink of nothingness was just as great as mine. But he was far more determined.

The roof of the passage was not high enough for us to stand the spars of the bridge in the grooves and lower the far end by ropes. So we mounted the near end on a pair of wheels and kept up the far end at an angle of forty-five degrees by pulling on a rope. Maria pushed this contraption forward or acted as brake if we raised it too high. When we finally dropped the bridge into position, axle and wheels went over the edge. We never heard a sound after the first bounce.

Maria greeted the accident with a merry laugh. She was perfectly happy standing a foot from the edge, and after all the old wheels weren't worth anything. She strolled about on the bridge with plump unconcern. Jim and I went over it on our hands and knees.

After a few yards the passage opened out into an irregular rock chamber too large for the beams of our flashlights to explore. The senhora, becoming the weaker sex again, remained at the entrance with a flashlight of her own. She didn't like that place at all.

Working our way around the walls, we had just decided that this was the end of the cave with no way out of it, when Maria let out a piercing scream. She had sat down with her back against the rock and a pool of light in front of her to keep off the bogeys. She stretched out her left hand to make herself more comfortable and placed it on the face of a corpse.

We rushed over to her. The dead man was a

Spaniard or Portuguese of the early sixteenth century. Body, clothes, and weapons were well preserved in the still, dry air. He was on his back, with arms crossed on his chest. He knew he had had it and laid himself down to die with dignity, trusting in the mercy of God. And there in the dust, undisturbed since his last unsteady steps, were the marks of his loose boots.

He had taken a sword or dagger thrust low down on the side of the throat. I should not have noticed the perforation of the mummified skin if the linen of his shirt had not been dark with dried blood.

It wasn't the expert, the scholar trained to facts and nothing but facts, who saw the vital bearing of a four-hundred-year-old murder on the problem of the ivory puma. It was Jim, of course, Jim with his passion for never destroying the record of the past through avoidable carelessness.

"We can find aht what 'appened, Mr. Penkivel, guv'," he said. "Spend a bit of time on it, and we don't 'ave to be Sherlock 'Olmeses."

He was right. The pointed, rather feminine tracks, though the edges were blurred, were utterly unlike our own and told the story. Two men had crossed the chasm. Side by side they walked to the far right-hand corner of the cave. There the dust was thoroughly trampled and disturbed as if they had been removing something, which they carried away. On their way back to the bridge the man walking a little behind had stabbed the other.

186

The murderer's footprints had been overlaid by ours and were muddied anyway, but a set of clean impressions, which we found pointing to the gap, seemed unexpectedly deep and firm. My astonishing collaborator was not content with a "seemed." He measured the depth of the heel prints. No doubt about it at all. The murderer when he left the inner cave was weighted down by his comrade's burden as well as his own.

The movements of the other were equally clear. When he fell forward, he left impressions of his knees and body. About where his neck would have been a patch of dust was caked by blood. Badly wounded or dying, he had then risen to his feet, staggered to where Maria nearly sat on him, and crossed his hands on his breast.

You see why. Because the trusted companion who had stabbed him from behind made doubly sure of him by destroying the bridge. So he lay down to wait for the end. No weeping and cursing on the edge of that uncrossable abyss for him. His simple act made me understand the contemporaries of Cortes and Pizarro as no books could. Probably he had the sense to see that the sword had been merciful, that he had not long to live. Even so, I think that if the corpse had been mine, it would have been found on the brink of the chasm with arms outstretched and mouth open.

I could now make a plausible guess at how the ivory puma came to be in the outer cave. The murderer, repacking his loot, had got rid of it as an ob-

187

ject of no value and inconvenient bulk. But it pleased him. He was a man of the Renaissance. I like to think of him as an Italian. So he stood it on the rock ledge instead of just throwing it away.

We found no concrete evidence of what the valuables had been. Maria with her quick fingers helped us to sift the dust. Nothing. Not even a spilled coin. But there was no need to drag in Atlantis. Boxes of gold and silver must often have gone astray in those days when the treasure fleets called at the Azores on their homeward voyage from the Spanish Main. The two adventurers, I suggested, could have been removing a hoard of stolen loot from the cave.

Jim did not deny it. He didn't stick to his lost continent. He merely pointed out, as modestly as the more courteous type of Oxford don, that I was ignoring inconvenient facts without explaining them. " 'Ow about the footprints of the blokes what put it there?" he asked.

I hadn't thought of that. Obviously the prints of the blokes who put it there—whatever "it" was— were not visible at the time of the murder, or they would be visible still. So in the sixteenth century they had already been obliterated by slow time. In that case, the treasure had been put in the cave long before the Azores were discovered.

By now I was unconsciously treating Jim as an authority. I suspect that my voice echoed through the darkness in a genuine academic falsetto as I tried to answer his question by complicated theories involving drafts of air cut off by the fallen boulder. But I had to admit that the case for Atlantis could not be finally dismissed.

You would have thought he'd have jumped at it and driven home another point, too—that the chiseled footings we had found suggested a permanent bridge, not the casual construction that would have been thrown across the abyss by two fearless conquistadors hiding or seeking a hoard of loot.

Jim stuck to the evidence, however, and nothing but the evidence. He squatted on the floor sucking his teeth, and then he blew his own beloved Atlantis sky-high.

"Them two was puttin' somethink in," he said, "not takin' it aht!" And he fiddled around some more in the marks of the heels with flashlight and foot ruler.

He was on to the truth. The tracks that led from the entrance to the disturbed corner were deeper than the tracks that led back to the site of the murder. So there it was. The two men *were* putting something in. They did not find a treasure in the inner cave at all. They carried it in across their bridge and dumped it.

So far, so good. But if that was what really happened, the murderer had to return from his victim to the corner in order to pick up the two loads and make off with them. And his tracks must still be there.

They were. Along the wall all the way. That's why we had missed them. Reconstruction was easy. Torch or candle had gone out in the struggle, so the murderer felt his way back to the treasure around the wall. Wounded man also had a pistol—a fine one for its date—which may have influenced the cautious movements of the other.

"Not what you wanted, Jim," I said. "I'm sorry. But you're a lot better off."

"Fifty-fifty, Mr. Penkivel, sir," he answered sternly.

I knew he must have noticed it. There was nothing his eyes missed, though, of course, he could not know the value of the emerald set in the pommel of the dead man's sword. Nor could I in the beam of a flashlight. But it was worth a lot for its extraordinary size even if flawed, as it almost certainly had to be.

I turned his offer down flat. In proportion to his resources, Jim had contributed to an archaeological expedition more than any millionaire's fund ever dreamed of. He was entitled to the finds, if any.

And then that amazing man reflected doubtfully. "Would yer say we 'ad the right to take it aht, guv'? We're 'ere for knowledge, not treasure 'unting."

I assured him that there were plenty of sixteenth-century swords in the world, and that this was of no special value except for the emerald set roughly and strongly into the hilt. Safest place to keep it, I suppose.

Well, yes, I must admit it was a superb weapon. But I wanted Jim to have the emerald, and I didn't know enough about the Portuguese law of treasure trove to be sure that if he produced the sword and emerald as they were he would be allowed the value.

Take it from me—state museums don't like paying out when they can get something for nothing.

"Okay, guv'nor," he said. "Sell it for me when yer gets 'ome because I wouldn't know 'ow. And you 'ave the ivory puma for the museum."

Why isn't it on exhibition? I've told you. Because the blasted thing is impossible! It asks us to assume a lost culture with affinities to both Old World and New. Yes, naturally, I had it dated by the radio-carbon method. The very large elephant that supplied the ivory, died not later than 2000 B.C. Origin unknown. All we can say. Nothing surprising in that. Every great museum has some lovely thing in the basement, waiting for the day when our successors will know enough to be able to label it.

There was nothing in the cave worth recording. Jim and I decided to leave the body where it was and remove our bridge. Like a couple of idiots we talked of cementing a ring bolt into the roof so that we could support the far end while we pulled it back. Maria's feminine common sense soon dealt with that.

"But why not drop it down the hole?" she asked in her lilting Portuguese. "We can always make another."

It's the end of the story. Unsatisfactory, as I told you, except for Jim. I got him six thousand pounds for the emerald.

The chiseled bridge footings? Oh, those! Well, the romanticist—that's me—finds them so inexplicable

191

that he is reexamining (please keep it to yourself!) the case for Atlantis. The cold-blooded authority—that's Jim—suggested that our two adventurers made a solid bridge because they intended at some later date to bring over a heavy mule train of stuff that they did not want to risk losing.

Possible, but odd. Remember they only entered the inner cavern once. They never explored it at all while they were building their bridge or afterward. They carried in their mysterious loot straightway and dumped it. Doesn't that look as if the bridge was already there?

And doesn't it suggest a sudden, hasty decision, not the behavior of men stacking away valuables in a carefully chosen hiding place? My own guess is that they found the cave and the treasure at the same time. They didn't know what to do with such wealth, how to ship it and dispose of it. So they agreed to carry it into the inner cave for the moment and perhaps break down the bridge.

Where did they find it? In the outer cave, of course, where it had remained untouched ever since it was abandoned by desperate refugees from the sunken cities of the plain on the lost continent of Atlantis.